CW00691079

© Nathanaël AMAH, 2022(**J9CR2N2**)

1   Elvira PLYNN Greatness & Decadence
© *Nathanaël AMAH , 2022   NATHAM Collection*

From the same author :
(E-books & paper version)

- Somewhere in Vladivostok
- Harcèlement   *(éd. BOD)*
- Harassment   *(éd. BOD)*
- Acoso   *(éd. BOD)*
- Neith (La mystérieuse Nubienne)   *(éd. BOD)*
- The Nubian (The mysterious Neith)   *(éd. BOD)*
- Les macarons   *(éd. BOD)*
- Instants ultimes   *(éd. BOD)*
- Que dire de plus ?   *(éd. BOD)*
- Cousine !   *(éd. BOD)*
- Tu n'es pas la femme de l'homme
              que je suis   *(éd BOD)*
- The day after in London   *(éd BOD)*
- Londres : le jour d'après   *(éd BOD)*
- Ma dernière nuit en Sibérie   *(éd BOD)*
- My last night in Siberia   *(éd BOD)*
- Faces   *(éd BOD)*
- Facettes   *(éd BOD)*
- GESICHTER   *(éd BOD)*
- The fragrant book   *(éd BOD)*
- Le livre parfumé   *(éd BOD)*
- Que veux-tu entendre que je
      ne t'ai pas dit ?   *(éd BOD)*
- What do you want to hear that

Elvira PLYNN Greatness & Decadence

I haven't told you ?   *(éd BOD)*
- ROXILLE (une histoire étonnante) *(éd BOD)*
- ROXILLE (an amazing story)   *(éd BOD)*
-Elvira PLYNN (Grandeur & Décacence)
                                        (éd BOD)

Cover : Imaginary portrait
(based on a digital production by the author)

4   Elvira PLYNN Greatness & Decadence

ELVIRA   PLYNN

(*Greatness & Decadence*)

PART 1

(In Pursuit of the American Dream)

« The crime carries its own punishment. » *(Richard Brinsley SHERIDAN)*

Elvira PLYNN Greatness & Decadence

1

Church of the Madeleine in Paris.

It is 3 p.m.

Elvira PLYNN Greatness & Decadence

The funeral service is coming to an end.

A grandiose, dignified, moving ceremony.

The business world is widely represented to say a final farewell to one of their own.
In perfect French, the eulogy is delivered by Ann, the eldest daughter of the deceased, specially returned from the United States for the occasion, at the head of a large American delegation.

Eulogy that ends in these terms:

« … Who knew my father, knows what an exceptional man he was. He has dedicated his entire life to the success of his business. He perpetuated the name of the PLYNNs here in France and around the world. He loved my mother with a crazy love, an unequivocal love. He devoted all his energy to keeping our family in perfect cohesion. We were a united family until the departure of my beloved mother, called back too soon by the Lord. We didn't lack anything. We were loved by this father who went to join our mother in the kingdom of heaven...

Dad, kiss Mom for us. Tell her that we think of her and that we miss her cruelly.
Goodbye Dad!
I love you Dad. Take care !»

Robert and Shirley join Ann in front of the altar for a fraternal embrace.

They cry together. They need to hug each other. Here they are definitively orphans of father and mother. They know how much it hurts.
They are now in a melee with themselves and with their destiny. Their grief is immense. In her role as big sister, Ann tries to comfort them, but remains inconsolable.

Many moving testimonies recall the journey of the deceased since his arrival in France.

Relatives, friends, all united by the same pain, honor with their presence, this farewell ceremony.

In the front row, a widow, in a strict black suit, enhanced by a black capeline style stradivarius, dignified, inconsolable, tries to make a good face.

The children of the deceased, born of a first union, sit just behind. A declared desire not to appear alongside their father's "French" wife.

The funeral service ends with Rameau's hymn "La Nuit", performed with great fervor by a choir of handpicked opera singers.

The choir sings Jean-Philippe RAMEAU's hymn to the night:

« …
Oh night comes to bring to the earth,
the calm enchantment of your mystery,
the shadow that escorts you is so sweet,
so sweet is the concert of your voices
singing hope,
so great is your power turning everything
into a happy dream,
… »

A hymn that the deceased listened to on a loop in the days before his death.

In a deafening concert of bells, the coffin leaves the church for the final stage of the ceremony.

Hearse in the lead, the long procession of black limousines with drivers, leaves the church to the Père Lachaise cemetery, where Father Uschinghson, childhood friend of the deceased, especially from the United States, says a last prayer in English, before the burial.

Thus ends this hard and trying autumn day during which Joseph PLYNN was buried in this Parisian cemetery, alongside some celebrities, in accordance with his last wishes.

Reception in one of the lounges of the LUTECIA hotel in Paris where guests are invited to have a snack and a last drink in memory of their friend Joseph.

The opportunity for his children to see old family friends, who came directly from the United States.

In a corner of the lounge, sitting in a period

armchair, a glass of whiskey in hand, Joseph PLYNN's widow is surrounded by a few French friends who have come to support her in her ordeal.

Visibly seeking to stun herself to contain her sorrow, glass after glass, rasades of whiskey are swallowed. Thus, her drunkenness allows her to endure the contempt of her deceased husband's children.

Moreover, she knows that Robert, who is at the head of her late husband's business in France, intends to challenge the holograph will drawn up by his father a few months before his death.

2

Officially deceased of a cardiac arrest at the age of 75, Joseph PLYNN, arrived in France in the 60s, to set up a subsidiary of the company created by his father who very young, made a fortune in the food industry in the USA.

He was the only living child of his parents, not because he was an only son, but because his mother had died in childbirth at the birth of his sister, who had also not survived childbirth.

It's a well-kept secret, ignored by everyone, even by his own children Ann, Robert and Shirley.

He had barely known his mother. He suffered a lot from this absence. Therefore, throughout his life, his desire to create a strong family unit, to maintain this sacred bond against all odds within this protective fortress, was his guiding principle. For him, a family is a father, a mother, children and a lot of love.

Each birth was a trial for him: judging his presence obligatory at the birth of each of his children, praying to God that everything would go well. And when the newborn and mother are out of harm's way, he couldn't help but go to church to thank this God who took his mother and sister away from him. The same God he has hated time and time again in his moments of despair, those moments when he would give his own life to have the wise advice of a mother, the benevolent look of a loving mother, the hand of a mother, caressing the hair of her child to reassure him.

He knows more than anyone, what it is like not to grow up alongside a mother, a lack that the colored nurses in blue and white uniforms, at the service of the family, could not in any way fill throughout his childhood. This made him somewhat neurasthenic throughout his life, not knowing how to manifest in a spontaneous and visible way, his joy or his moods.

This introverted character that he retained until adulthood has singularly impacted his way of interacting with the outside world, especially in the way he conducts his business.

His interlocutors are often dismayed in front of this person who opposes them a complete illegibility on his face. Difficult then, to know the substance of his thought. He is someone who does not like to talk about rain and good weather, he is a man who decides without asking questions, sometimes leaving his interlocutors or friends totally speechless.

Some will say he is shy. Unless it is a shell allowing him to protect himself from the outside world. Nothing is less certain.

What is on the other hand a certainty and an astonishment, seen from within the family unit, is his ability to be, in the presence of his children, an attentive father, kind, open, cheerful, playful, laughing, ... In short, the most reassuring, even the most "normal" image of the good father.

His schooling was brief. Not because he was not good at studies, but because his father needed him for his business, to prepare him to succeed him.

Thus, with the High School Diploma in his pocket, he joined the family business, starting at the very bottom of the ladder.

From overseeing the storage of corn kernels to distributing bags of grain across the country, he knew all the ropes of the trade.

Subsequently, considerably enriched, his position granted him full powers within the company.

He proved to be a formidable and skilled negotiator.

Faced with the indisputable leadership of his son, John PLYNN has become by necessity, a simple advisor to this son who forces his admiration.

Very British in appearance but without the phlegm that goes with it, Joseph wears a thin mustache that has become graying over time.

In his hometown of Bowling Green (kentucky, the seat of Warren County), each of his appearances in the grounds of Baptist Church, stirred up the young suitors of the city, each claiming to belong to the best lineage in the region to claim to join the famous family of John PLYNN, the grain magnate.

Competing in strategies and postures, they exploited every opportunity to attract Joseph's benevolent gaze.

One day, during a charity fair, Barbara, the eldest daughter of the Reverend Pastor Gary Turner, with a straw hat on her head, is busy topping the lemon Poppyseed cakes with cream cheese frosting. She doesn't notice that the next customer in the queue is Joseph.

Big impression when she notices it.

He is there, in front of her, waiting wisely for his plate of cream cake.

How many young contenders would like to be in her place at this very moment? This is an opportunity to be seized and she has no intention of letting it pass.

Occupying a strategic position at the end of the chain behind the cake stand, she completes the action of her friend Jenny, in charge of slicing the cakes before passing her the plates for the topping. Therefore, she cannot make herself available for a bit of chat with the seductive Joseph.

How to do it?

A double ration of cream?

No !

Too visible. What to do to get noticed without looking like it?

Suddenly, a genius idea ran through her mind.

As she hands him the plate, she looks him straight in the eye. She whispers something inaudible to him, forcing him to wonder.

He doen't have to be a specialiar in the language of the deaf and dumb to decipher the words on her lips.

Yes, he read very clearly on her lips:

« *I love you* ».

He didn't dream.

In addition, this girl with the straw hat keeps staring into his eyes, creating in him, a feeling of unease, which is unfamiliar to him until this precise moment.

It passes or it breaks, she tells to herself. Never mind her status as a pastor's daughter.

At first, Joseph is puzzled. He feels destabilized. He doesn't know what to do to meet the challenge.

What reaction to what seems totally new to him? What to do in the face of this creature that no one would call brazen? How to react to this daring gesture that is part of the magic of the moment?

No woman had ever approached him in the past, and for him, it is a situation that is not ordinary.

So, he timidly reaches out to receive his plate of cream cake. And in a shy voice, he says:

« *Thanks !* »

Then he adds:

« *Who are you ?* »

« ***Barbara   Turner, sir***». she says.

Then, he walks away from the stand without adding anything, without looking back.

She feels shabby that she has not been able to make him perceive the intensity of her desire to get his attention.

But she is wrong.

From that strange moment, against all odds a few months later, the Reverend Gary Turner celebrated his daughter Barbara's union with Joseph PLYNN to the despair of all the other suitors of the county.

From this union were born three children.

3

When he arrived in France, it was love at first sight for this country that he discovered for the first time.

At school, he had vaguely heard about the landing on the Normandy coast. For many deep America americans, Europe in general and France in particular are an abstraction. For them, the world stops at the geographical limits of the USA.

From then on, he settled permanently in France with his wife Barbara, his children Ann, Robert and Shirley, who came to join him a few months later.

Because of their passion for horses, their first establishment was Chantilly, about fifty kilometers from Paris, in a restored property of the eighteenth century, in the middle of a closed park.

Chantilly is a town in the Oise department in northern France.

This town is located in the heart of the forest of Chantilly, in the valley of the Nonette.

It is located in the centre of an agglomeration of about 37,000 inhabitants.

A racecourse completes the landscape, between the state high school and the large stables.

Two major events take place there each year: the Prix de Diane and the Prix du Jockey Club, two world-famous horse races.

Diane's prize is the most glamorous equestrian event of the season. The opportunity for the women of the good old Cantilian society to adorn themselves with the best finery: elegance, extravagance, sartorial madness. Everything goes there.

In this city, everything reminds them of the American West, a mustang region in particular. The forest, the cult of the horse, nothing is missing.

The state of Kentucky where Joseph PLYNN is from, is a large horse breeding area. His father, old John, owned for several years, a breeding of racehorses, known throughout the world, for the excellence and lineage of his horses. He knew better than anyone, to cross the genetics of his horses to obtain the best results: dresses, velocity, endurance. In summary, the best of the horse breed.

When his father died, Joseph sold this farm to his cousin who had been John's assistant for several years, to devote himself solely to the agri-food sector.

Ann and her brother Robert, who knew how to ride a horse before knowing how to walk, assiduously frequented the large stables of the Chantilly estate, one of the largest stables in Europe, built by the architect Jean Aubert for Louis-Henri de Bourbon, 7th Prince of Condé.

These riding sessions, which take place at the resumption of Thursday afternoon, are an opportunity to meet the children of the local nobility. On the other hand, it is also an opportunity to meet this American family who came to settle in the region.

Thus, bonds of friendship were gradually created between the PLYNN and many Cantilian families of the town and the surrounding area.

The many garden parties organized in the PLYNN park also are events not to be missed.

Ms Barbara's cakes are legendary, Joseph's word.

Over time, Robert PLYNN, the youngest son,

succumbed to the charms of a sweet Cantilian named Sylvie, a lawyer by profession, whom he married a few years later.

From this union were born five children.

4

Barbara, professional teacher before in america, « brazen » daughter of the highly esteemed and very respected Pastor Gary Turner, occasionally works in the reception cell of the congregation of the American Church of Paris, while continuing to assume her role as a wife. She tries to maintain within her home, the spirit of the typical American family, both in terms of the education of children and that of everyday life.

The beginning of meals is systematically preceded by benedicity, called in turn, in English.

The education of her children is strict.

Barbara does her best to save her three children from this wind of freedom that is beginning to blow over France.

May 68 is not far away.

It must be remembered that Barbara was born and raised in the United States.

In the 60s, American Puritanism is more generally, a religious state of mind strongly and durably marked by the austerity of morals.

The notion of the individual responsibility of the believer before God, without the intermediary of any moral or religious authority, (clergy or otherwise), which would be invested with a divine mission, is a reality.

Thus, considering the strong influences of presbyterian, Methodist, Baptist, Quaker and many other religious structures flourishing in the United States at that time, it is clear that the Puritan spirit does not belong to a defined religious denomination.

Moreover, to the extent that not all Americans are passionate about theology and burn the same ardent faith, Puritanism is a true life choice.

This observation is all the more true because it illustrates the most astonishing and the most disconcerting peculiarity of the United States that integrates religion into everyday life, making religion an integral part of social life.

The religious spirit, the permanent reference to God, the notions of Good and Evil, are the guideline of the majority of people.

Barbara is one of this majority of people, even though she resides more than eight thousand kilometers from her native land.

Ann and her siblings endured this dictatorship of religion throughout their lives alongside their mother.

If, deep down, she sometimes feels torn between the shackles of religion and the appreciation of the flavors of life in the face of the irresistible attraction for the things of "ordinary" life, Barbara remains no less a woman, with women's desires.

For her, coitus is not synonymous with procreation, but must be considered as a human relationship, requiring de facto, much more than one individual in a sexually human behavior.

One of the many questions that remain unanswered in her mind:

When must she make the sign of the cross? Before or after coitus?

Stupid and simple question at the same time that she never managed to ask either her father or her pious mother, the wife of the Honorable Pastor Turner.

Why this fear? Why this need to know?

So, in order not to have everything wrong before God, she makes the sign of the cross before and after.

With a man whose sexual experience is very limited, almost non-existent, Barbara did not choose in the person of Joseph, the right half to compose her couple.

She defines herself as a sulphurous woman, says one of her friends.

Sulphurous?   Yes, but to what extent?

What is certain, however, at the time of her marriage, she is a charming young American girl, without the assurance that most young girls of her age and condition testify. Perhaps because of her young age, 20 years old, and the particular subtlety of her character. She aspires to become a woman in all her fullness, a little serious, a little sulphurous, a little sensual, a little delicate, a little cheeky, ...

She did not hold an approved record for the number of lovers in the county. But, in herself, she feels the need to feel alive, with this irrepressible desire to defy the prohibitions, even if her morality as a good Christian prevents her from being that woman she delights in looking at in the mirror.

5

Since their arrival in France, several years have passed.

PLYNNs live the perfect happiness.

The children's schooling is going well. Joseph's business is at the top level. Joseph PLYNN is a rich man.

The children are fulfilled and have become

perfectly bilingual, even though Barbara demands that English be the usual language at home.

Initially, Joseph opposed it. But he eventually understood his wife's point of view. It is important not to forget the motherland. The soul of the American family must subsist beyond borders.

Barbara does not care about the need for her family to integrate into a society that is not her own. For now, they live in France, but tomorrow: where will they be?

For her, the integration of foreigners into a society other than that of their origins cannot be done objectively. Can water and oil be mixed? she replies when the question is put to her. The juxtaposition of several cultures cannot give a homogeneous mixture. On the other hand, assimilating the habits and customs of the country in which one lives is a vital necessity, even a real asset.   .

The mixing of their two ways of life seems to give good results. She does not complain, as long as the children are happy.

From time to time, conflicts break out within the family between Barbara and the children.

One of the causes: the "Europeanized" attitude of children that goes against Barbara's "Americanized" recommendations. Joseph is reduced, in his role as a father, to settle this type of conflict all the time, he, the fervent defender of positive diversity.

Every summer, they happily return to Kentucky. They reunite with relatives and long-time friends.

Ann has returned to an old flirtation. They talk about engagement. They want to celebrate it in France.

Jerry (the happy suitor) has heard so much about French romanticism that, simply announcing to his friends his upcoming engagement that will be celebrated in France, would undoubtedly propel him to the top of his popularity.

But when Barbara returned from this last summer spent in Kentucky, she felt very tired. Violent and stubborn headaches do not leave her.

Initially, the focus is on travel fatigue and jet lag. It is true that Barbara spared no effort during the last stay in Kentucky. So many things to do, so many visits to make, so many receptions to organize. Etc...

A little rest should be enough to put everything in order, concludes the neighborhood doctor consulted at his office.

A few weeks later, things don't seem to be going back to normal as planned.

On the contrary, they are getting worse.

Barbara loses weight in plain sight.

She is overcome by generalized fatigue that prevents her from getting up. She spends most of her time in bed or in a lounge chair in front of the TV, unable to make the slightest effort.

She can hardly eat on her own. The assistance of a nurse became necessary.

Joseph decides to have her transported to a Parisian hospital.

Extensive analyses are carried out.

The results reveal a widespread viral infection.

Joseph does not understand. They have never been to a tropical country. Their last stay abroad (if one can consider their home country as a foreign country for them), was in Kentucky as usual.

At the insistence of the chief medical officer of the hospital to which Barbara has been admitted for a week, to find out what changed in their habits during their last vacation in Kentucky, Joseph remembers a lunch on the banks of the Nolin River Dam Lake, not far from Brownsville.

It was one of those days when the heat was

overwhelming and unbearable. As soon as they arrived, the PLYNN family settled in for a picnic. But before lunch, Barbara felt the need to take a dip in the cool water.

After several minutes in the cool water of the lake, Barbara ended her swim to dry in the sun before serving lunch on the grass.

This is the only highlight of this last vacation in the country that he remembers. It was all the more curious that Barbara was the only one who wanted to swim that day in the lake.

Joseph suddenly became aware of the possibility of contamination in the water of the lake.   But nothing is certain.

The last exams are very bad. Barbara's liver is attacked and requires the transplant of a healthy liver.

She is placed in intensive care while waiting to find a donor.

But, her condition deteriorates very quickly.

At the end of the second week spent in the hospital, Barbara passed away in the early morning at the age of 52, not surrounded by the affection of her family. She left, without being able to say goodbye to them.

6

According to her last wishes, Barbara's ashes were brought back to Kentucky to be scattered in Mammoth Cave National Park around the giant sequoia, a few miles from Bowling Green.

Back in France, Joseph and his children are still reeling from Barbara's abrupt departure. The dazzling nature of her illness, which led to her death, left them speechless. They are flabbergasted. They find it difficult to get out of this state of denial: Barbara's belongings have remained as they are, in their usual place. At the table, nothing has changed. Her chair is not occupied, as if, back from the kitchen, she will come to settle down to share the meal with them. The void she has left is immense. They are inconsolable.

Ann decided to return to live in the United States, as soon as her father was able to bear her absence after her mother's.

Robert, who has been promoted to managing director of the company, will remain in France to manage the business in which all children are now associated. Shirley doesn't know what she plans to do yet.

Months have passed.

Life went on.

Business is still thriving.

The property of the eighteenth century, seems

to have found a certain serenity, although the memory of Barbara is omnipresent in the house. All say they saw her at least once between two doors, wandering, going about her business as before, as if nothing had happened. Footsteps sometimes resonate on the floor in the middle of the night. Other times, it is sobs that tear the silence of the night apart.

One fine morning, Joseph (still inconsolable), finally resigns himself and decides to take a long vacation with one of his French friends who owns a property on the heights of Grasse in the south of France, a city that rises to 300 meters above sea level.

A complete change of scenery for Joseph who discovers for the first time the Maritime Alps and its surroundings that he had heard a lot about.

He does not know where to turn. He is as if intoxicated in front of these new landscapes that are offered to him.

He frequents Cannes assiduously, which is

only about fifteen kilometers north of Grasse.

He runs the vernissages, he visits the museums.
He is interested in the perfume industry. He is thinking of creating a fragrance for his late wife.
Discussions are well advanced.

He discovers the pleasure of going to the open market on Saturday morning.

He tried his hand at cooking, concocting Provençal dishes inspired by recipe books bought from the bookseller in his neighborhood, with whom he became friends.

Barbara would be surprised to see him cooking, he who did not know how to cook a hard-boiled egg.

He wrote a thousand and one letters to his children to tell them about his daily life in Grasse.

He keeps an eye on the management of the company and takes stock with Robert every

Monday morning.

Gradually, his excitement of the first days subsided to give way to a deep melancholy.

He bitterly regrets the absence of Barbara with whom he would have liked to make all these discoveries.

He imagines her surprise at the moment of offering her this perfume specially created for her.

His surprise would have been twofold.

Joseph is not used to giving gifts. Curiously, he considers that everyone can afford what he wants by drawing on the funds made available to the family. It is his conception of the pleasure of having fun. Only everyone knows what to offer to have fun.

On the other hand, with great emotion, she will be able to measure her husband's love for her by perpetuating her memory through this fragrance that would be dedicated to her forever.

He hears her voice, telling him:

*"**Oh !!!! Thank you so very much my darling** . "*

A month later, on a Saturday morning, market day. Joseph is in front of his favorite fishmonger's stall.

He wisely queues.

It is now his turn.

The fishmonger (in English with a perfect accent from the south of France):

« ***Good morning Sir !*** »

Joseph (with a broad smile) :

« ***Good morning my friend !*** »

The fishmonger, whose English is limited to these three words, adds in French:

« ***What are your desires this morning?*** »

Joseph points to the shells, saying:

45   Elvira PLYNN Greatness & Decadence

« *Scallops?* »

The fishmonger:
« ***Non, ce sont des noix de pétoncle*** » (No Sir).

Joseph (doubtful) asks in french :

« ***Pétanque ?*** »   (*Petanque ?*)

The fishmonger bursts out laughing, then:

« ***No Sir ! P E T O N C L E !!! the cousin of the scallop. Got it?*** »

Joseph tries to understand. He doesn't know what to answer.

A few seconds later, the person who follows him in the queue, blows him in english without an accent:

« *Scallop nuts* »

He turns around and sees a young woman with a closed face.

Joseph :

« **Oh Thanks !** »

« *You're welcome.* » replies the young lady sketching a slight smile.

After placing his order, and while the fishmonger prepares his crustaceans, Joseph turns to the young lady:

« *American ?* »

The young lady :

« *No, French* »

Joseph :

« *Oh glad to meet you !* »

« *Glad to meet you !* » replies the young lady.

7

Joseph retrieves his bags.

He steps back to give the young woman the opportunity to get closer to the stall.

A few moments later, she in turn retrieves her bags of fish and shellfish.

Joseph approaches her and introduces himself:

« *Joseph* !»

The young lady :

« *Pleased to meet you !* »

Then :

« *Elvira !* »

« *How do you do ?* »   replies Joseph.

« *Do you live in this area?* » asks Joseph.

 « *I'm living in the heights of Grasse. And you?* »   replies Elvira.

« *Oh ! What a coincidence. Me too.*» replies Joseph with great enthusiasm.

« *Do you speak french, Joseph ?* » asks Elvira.

« *A little bit ! Not as fluent as you speak english. You have the advantage over me.* » replies Joseph a little embarrassed.

« *No, you express yourself very well. I have no merit, I lived a few years in New York with my first husband. When he died, I came back to live in France, in Grasse, in our property. ... And what do you do in the region?* » asks Elvira.

« *After my wife passed away a few months ago, almost a year ago now, I worked hard to occupy my mind. For a month, I have been living in the property of my French friend on the heights of Grasse to recharge my batteries and forget my sorrow...* » explains Joseph in a hesitant french, and with a little sadness in his voice.

« *I understand you Joseph. ... We would like life to stop. ... But in the end, life goes on and time does its work. ... That's why I preferred to come back to live in France.* » explains Elvira.

« *Do you have children ?* » asks Joseph.

« *No, unfortunately. My late husband underwent very aggressive chemo that made him sterile.* » confesses Elvira.

« *Cancer ?* » asks Joseph.

« *Yes! Testicular cancer.* » confesses Elvira.

« *Oh God !!! He suffered a lot … the poor man !* » says Joseph , very compassionate.

Elvira stays silent, visibly sad.

« *May we have a drink ?* » asks Joseph.

Elvira slows down, turns her head, and stares at Joseph for a short moment.
Then:

« *Oh Sure ! The heat becomes stifling.* »

That said, they settle on the terrace of the first bistro at the exit of the market.

Sitting face to face, everyone unpacks the story of their life.

In the interval of an eyelash beat, each knows everything about the other.

Thus, Elvira learns that Joseph is the heir of the PLYNN cereals, recent widower, three adult children, etc ... .

Hummm !!! very interesting !

For his part, Joseph does not know much more about her.

One point puzzles him : impossible to know the name of her late husband.

Even more astonishing: total impossibility of knowing in which neighborhood she lived in New York.

For now, it doesn't matter. The main one, to make a chat with this unknown woman who saved his life in front of the stall of the fishmonger.

He thinks back to scallop nuts. Then:

« *Do you know how to prepare scallop nuts?* » asks Joseph.

« *Of course it is! There is nothing simpler....*

Joseph, here's what we're going to do: entrust me with your scallop nuts, and come and enjoy them tonight at my house at the villa. ... That's an honest proposal, isn't it? .... What do you think? » she said, her face suddenly radiating with happiness, becoming aware of this angle of attack that has come providentially to offer itself to her as on a silver platter.

Who would have believed it?

Long live the PETONCLES!!!

8

Joseph complied and entrusted her with his precious scallop nuts.

Elvira gave him her address and took leave.

After Elvira leaves, Joseph stays for a while on the terrace of the bistro. He orders another glass.

He feels a little guilty to have accepted the invitation of this stranger.

Too quickly for his taste.

Then starts an imaginary conversation with Barbara, who seems to warn him against the lightness of his decision.

Which danger is there to go to taste scallop nuts ? he retorts to her.

I will have warned you, retorts Barbara.

He finishes his glass and returns to the property.

During the afternoon, whereas he took the habit of making a small nap after his lunch, it is impossible for him to close the eye.

His mind is populated by an interminable series of questions which torments him since his meeting with Elvira:

when does one know that one has made his mourning?

How do you know when it's time to open your heart again, bruised by a brutal separation?

Can one feel the appeasement of the heart when the memory of the beloved one is still so vivid in oneself ?

After all, whose fault is it ?

The one who cowardly abandoned the other to his or her sad fate?

Or to the one who knew how to overcome his or her pain during the so-called "regulatory" or even "socially convenient" period, in order to finally turn the page and tell the men and women that it is time to rejoin the world of the living?

In an indescribable hubbub, Joseph's brain finally found the appeasement that allowed him to doze for an hour or two.

He did not have the courage to write his daily letter to his children. That can wait until Monday.

Yet the story of the scallop nuts could have fascinated them.

But, does he really want to tell them this story, the whole story, from A to Z?

And thus to reveal himself in front of his children at the moment when his life is about to take its course.

He knows that with regard to Barbara, there was never the slightest shadow in the picture of his feelings for her.

His attachment to his wife from the fair stand to that fateful day of her departure to the Lord, has never known weakness.

He doesn't remember having a single argument with her.

Everything went together with her.

He loved life with her.

But today, the meeting with Elvira has left

him with a strange impression. It is a strange feeling that allows him to see himself in the position of a person in demand. As if for the first time he is the initiator of an important event in the making. He did not forget the very special way Barbara used to attract his attention. That was very effective, since it is *in fine*, she who won his heart among all the pretenders of the county of Warren.

At the bottom, what he would have wanted, he?

Not to feel short-circuited in his role of the male who, by definition, must be in charge? On the initiative?

He realizes that this is a frustration that he has carried for his entire life. This has not prevented him from being a good husband and a good father. He is convinced to have loved Barbara with a sincere love.

Anyway!

It's time to get ready.

9

With a bouquet of red roses in his hand, Joseph arrived at the villa's door at the appointed hour.

He rings the bell with a sharp knock.

A few moments later, a click triggers the opening of the gate equipped with a surveillance camera.

He enters the property, crosses an alley paved with pink granite in accordance with the façade of the villa.

It is a beautiful building, flowered and very well maintained.

He approaches the front door.

It opens.

In the embrasure, Elvira in all her splendor.

She is dressed of a long dress, in cotton and of pearly pink color.

Her neck and her ears are naked. Her feet also, revealing long fine toes with varnished nails.

He can now see the color of her eyes, previously hidden behind big sunglasses during the meeting at the market.

He does not have the impression to be in the presence of the same person met a few hours before.

This can be explained by the phenomenon of transfiguration that takes place in the natural environment of an individual.

An individual at home is not the same outside.

He reassures himself as he can.

Finally, for him, nothing to report! It is an invitation, only an invitation to taste scallop nuts.

Elvira invites him inside and closes the door behind her.

Joseph hands her the roses.

She accepts them without saying a word, and goes to the kitchen to put them in a pot.

Joseph, who had not been invited to sit down, remained standing at the entrance to the living room, sweeping his gaze across the room containing tasteful and richly decorated furniture.

It is the first time in his entire life that he finds himself locked up with a woman about whom he knows almost nothing, and who seems to subjugate him to the highest degree.

For him, it is a special day.

While seeing her moving away towards the kitchen with the bouquet of roses in the hand, Joseph could not help observing through her walk intentionally swayed, her posterior which does not leave him indifferent.

Elvira returns to the living room with the roses skilfully arranged in a vase of color ruby, which really emphasizes them, vase that she puts delicately on the central pedestal table.

Then she walks over to Joseph, gives him a kiss on the cheek and says:

"*Thank you!*"

Joseph sketches a smile. He is confused. He seems to stammer something between his lips, like:

"*You're welcome!*"

She takes him by the hand and leads him to the sofa and invites him to sit down.

She walks back to the kitchen with the same swaying gait.

A few moments later, she comes back with a champagne bucket filled with a bottle of that expensive champagne.

She invites Joseph to work.

A little awkward at first, Joseph finally manages to pop the cork followed by a geyser of the precious nectar.

She hurriedly presented the glasses to minimize the loss, collecting a few drops on her fingers that she passed behind Joseph's ears and behind hers.

"*French tradition? A lucky charm?*" asks Joseph.

*"**Sure ! It will bring us happiness.** "* replies Elvira.

*"**Yes! It will bring us happiness**"*.

Ah? "Us" ?

A small detail that has its importance. But for the time being, Joseph seems to appreciate this cocoon in which he finds himself.

Some would see through this idyllic picture, the black widow, patiently weaving her web around a male who has succumbed to her pheromones.

Hardly the first sips absorbed, Elvira invites him to visit her villa.

Room after room, his glass of champagne in hand, Joseph can realize the incredible luxury in which his hostess evolves.

He is impressed. A delight for the eyes.

The visit finally ends.

They come back to settle on the sofa.

10

Elvira suggests that the dinner be held in the kitchen.

Joseph does not object.

Installed at the kitchen table decorated with an authentic mosaic by the famous Belgian-Luxembourgish artist Marleen Lacroix, Joseph religiously listens to Elvira's explanations about the recipe she has chosen to prepare his scallop nuts.

Juggling the utensils like a professional in front of Joseph's amazed eyes, Elvira finishes the presentation of the scallop nuts flambéed with cognac, accompanied by rice lightly perfumed with curry.

Elvira takes her place at the kitchen table, fills the glasses again with champagne and tell him:

"*Enjoy your meal!*"

At the first bite, Joseph exclaims:

"*Oh my goodness!!!*"

Elvira can't hide her joy.

She is on top of her glory.

Joseph has just taken the bait.

Now how to hook him and get him out of the water? ... (To be continued!)

The end of the dinner takes place in a religious silence, punctuated by the soft sound of cutlery on the plates.

Everything seems to indicate that everything is going well.

Joseph asks for more.

Elvira complies.

The bottom of the bottle of champagne is quickly reached. Elvira proposes another bottle, but suggests that they go to the living room to enjoy it after dinner.

Is Joseph in a position to refuse her anything?

Back in the living room after having put the kitchen in order, Elvira joins Joseph on the sofa.

Joseph accepts this rapprochement without putting up any resistance.

He feels good.

He hasn't felt this wellness for a long time. Not because the many glasses of champagne have changed his feeling, but simply because Elvira is a permanent source of enchantment since their meeting.

After a moment of silence, Joseph turns to his hostess and says:

"It was a real delight Elvira! Thanks so very much. I do not regret having given you my scallop nuts. ... It will be my pleasure to take cooking classes with you."

"We start tomorrow?" replies Elvira.

"Tomorrow and every other day." says Joseph.

"Be careful Joseph! I could take you at your word!" threatens Elvira.

"What have I said wrong?" Joseph worries.

"This is my way of saying that I feel at home. Nothing else." he adds.

*"**I too feel good with you, Joseph**"* confesses Elvira.

By joining the gesture to the word, Elvira gets a little closer to her guest.

Joseph does not know which attitude to adopt.

He hesitates between the restraint imposed on him by his status as a recent widower, and the liberation of his long-dormant male impulses.

Faced with this woman whose every gesture, every action, every intention, are so many pitfalls to avoid, curiously, Joseph feels a strong attraction towards her.

His body reacts to this visual stimulation to which is added a powerful olfactory signature, as his hostess gets closer to him on the sofa.

Elvira follows a well established plan.

There is no way Joseph will leave the villa

without a guarantee that he will return within the next few hours.

The clock is ticking.

Joseph glances at his watch.

11:45 p.m

He finishes his glass of champagne.

"*May I have a cab?*" he asks.

"*No way! I dop you at home*" she replies.

It's no longer time for jokes. It's time to strike back.

"*Do you really want to go home tonight?*" asks Elvira.

Surprised by the question, Joseph retorts:

"*We barely know each other ....*"

Putting on her saddest face, Elvira tries everything.

"*I do not want to leave you tonight. ... I no longer want to sleep alone in my big cold bed ... Stay with me! ... Please! Stay, please!*"

Then she adds, pretending to get up:

"*... If you really want to go home, just wait a second, I need to change my dress...*".

Joseph perceives her disappointment and the sadness in her voice. And at the fateful moment when she is about to get up, he holds her hand firmly.

11

On the morning of their first night, Elvira and Joseph wake up huddled together.

Joseph is doubtful: how can he suspect this woman, so sweet, so cuddly, of having bad intentions against him, she who has just offered him a memorable night?

Even if, at this precise moment, he does not

know her real name and surname, nor the district where she lived in New York, it does not make her a woman of bad life, a woman to be avoided at all costs.

Since Barbara's departure several months have passed. He does not have the impression to have betrayed the memory of his late wife by sleeping with this woman met the day before at the market. On the contrary!

But, what has just happened during this torrid night in which he actively took part, does not sound for all that the end of his mourning.

Indeed, how to forget this woman at the same time impetuous, impertinent, good mother of family and exceptional lover at her hours?

During these last months, this question has never haunted his mind, nor populated his thoughts.

For him, life has taken its course and must continue its course. He feels it is a vital necessity.

His family, his business, all demand his attention at all times.

He has never shirked his responsibilities. It is not in his nature.
The education he has received has installed in him this will to always do the right thing at the right time.

He knows that he has been an exemplary husband during the short time (what is 25 years in the scale of universal time?) during which he lived with Barbara in Kentucky and Chantilly.

Now that his instincts as a living being are awakening, why should he feel guilty about giving free rein to his impulses?

Besides, who can condemn him?

His children?

He does not believe it.
Ann went back to live in the United States. She has her own life. She is almost married to Jerry with whom she lives in a marital relationship. Barbara would not have liked

this situation. But she is not there any more to rectify the situation and to make it more suitable, more acceptable, socially speaking.

Robert has taken on the role of General Manager, which fits him like a glove.
He is a man, like his father, of exemplary rectitude, a gifted businessman and, moreover, a person who does not like to look into the plate of his table neighbor.
His motto: everyone does what they want, but with respect for the other.

As for Shirley, the youngest, what can she reproach her father who has always agreed with her?

She chose the Fine Arts while Barbara wanted her to become a nurse.

She dated a young painter, much to Barbara's despair, who could not conceive that her daughter could have a penchant for another girl.

It was an unbearable situation for her.

Joseph always supported his daughter against Barbara's wishes, even when she came out to him on the day of the presentation of her lover to her family.

It was one of the few times when the beautiful spirit of the American family that had always reigned in their home almost shattered.

Shirley made her father, her most valuable ally.

Is he lost in conjecture?

What if all this reasoning is only a view of his mind and not an absolute certainty?

Some could consider that the night he has just spent with Elvira, at Elvira's house, in Elvira's bed, is the first step of his reconstruction. Even if, seen from the outside, the alteration of his judgment by the fine bubbles of champagne and the expert fingers of his hostess, makes no doubt.

The necessary opening towards the other,

does not have vocation to put an end to his pain.

It ratifies his will to be reconciled with LIFE.

He feels ready to consider a new life.

Therefore, logically, a new love encounter could be on the agenda for the next few months.

To know the joy of loving again, and to experience the delights of happiness in a couple where love would be the only rule: he starts to dream about it after this night spent with Elvira.

12

Reflections of short duration.

Elvira invites him to take a bath.

He accepts it. How to resist to such an invitation ?

Moment of relaxation which closes this

unexpected but nevertheless very pleasant night.

Elvira slips into the bathroom in her little clothes.

She wants to help him to wash himself.

Joseph lets her: he has not known this pleasure that all children know with their moms.

From the bathtub, he goes into the shower cabin with multiple jets, in which he is rinsed, massaged and toned.

Joseph observes and experiences all this with delight.

Elvira does not show herself more enterprising than it is necessary to be towards her guest who expects a little more.

He begins to take taste to the thousand and one attentions of his hostess.

Before going to deposit him at his place, they

spend a moment together in the kitchen around a cup of coffee.
Elvira takes advantage of this moment to remind him how much she feels happy with him.

She does not make too much of it, but lets foresee her disappointment to have to separate from him.

Back home at the property, Joseph settles on the sofa.

He tries to wake up from this waking dream in which he would like to stay forever.

It's been two days since he last wrote to his children.

So he tries to do so now by going to his office.

He can't get two words together: the ideas don't come. Or at least, he doesn't know what to say?

An hour passes. Still nothing.

He tries again and again.

Then he decides to call Robert on the phone to tell him that he has decided to extend his stay in Grasse.

Big surprise in Chantilly. But ...

He takes the opportunity to bring forward the Monday meeting. Not much to say. Everything goes well.

Robert does not recognize his father. He feels that something is going on, but he doesn't dare to question him.

He tries a poker game.

*"**Dad, may I come to visit you on next weekend? I need to move a bit. Yes?"** he* says.

 After a moment of silence, and against all odds :

"***Of course, but come with your sister***".

"***Ok Dad! Thanks. Take care***" replies Robert.

"***You too! Bye!***" replies Joseph.

Robert receives this agreement as a sign of an important event.

13

After hanging up with his father, Robert starts to think.

He calls his sister.

"*We're going to Grasse at the end of the week.*"

"*What for?*" asks Shirley.

"*Dad wants to see both of us*" answers Robert.

"*Ah? What's going on? Did you just talk to him?*" says Shirley.

"*Yes, he sounded very cryptic to me.*" Robert adds.

"*Do you think he wants to introduce us to his new fiancée?*" kidding Shirley.

"*Stop the nonsense!*" replies Robert.

"*You'll see!*" continues Shirley.

Robert sees the possibility after all. It's possible that his father could have met a woman there, and with whom he would consider starting a new life.

"*How long has it been since Mom left?*" asks Robert.

"*It was yesterday...*" replies Shirley.

"*Yes!*" replies Robert with a heavy sigh.

*"**Do you think the giant redwood is doing better since Mom enriched its land?**"* asks Shirley as she remembers her mother's last trip to her homeland.

*"**Probably yes!**"* replies Robert, who also remembers that poignant moment.

He especially remembers the time that stood still as Barbara's ashes were spread around the giant redwood tree.

The park, normally teeming with people, was momentarily empty of any soul around the giant sequoia. It was as if the giant redwood had irradiated the immediate area so that no one could come and pervert and disturb the place at the precise moment when it, (the giant redwood), was receiving Barbara, the daughter of the country, back home to stay forever.

Shirley has also noticed it.

She is invaded by a deep sadness, she who never evoked this moment with anybody before.

Back in her room, she spent hours crying.

Then she fell asleep with the impression that her head was resting on her mother's thighs, and that her mother was gently running her fingers through her hair while singing her favorite lullaby:

"Baby's boat the silver moon,
Sailing in the sky,
Sailing over the sea of sleep,
While the clouds float by.

> *Sail, Baby, sail*
> *Out upon that sea,*
> *Only don't forget to sail*
> *Back again to me.*

Baby's fishing for a dream,
Fishing near and far,
His line a silver moonbeam is,
His bait a silver star."

14

« *Hello sister !* »

« *Shirley ? Everything is ok there ?* »

« *Is Jerry next to you ?* »

 « *Yes, why ? You are worring me !* »

 "*In that case, we'll speak French, if you like.*"

"*Okay, tell me, what's going on? Why all the*

Elvira PLYNN Greatness & Decadence

mystery? Is it Dad? Did something happen to him? Shirley, you can tell me, you know?"

After a moment of silence:

"I think Mom is really dead now ...."
whispers Shirley.

Ann is shocked and angry that she doesn't understand the significance of what is happening over there in France.

"That's enough !!!! What's going on?" yells Ann, nearly waking Jerry.

"I think Dad is getting married again"   tells Shirley her sister.

Ann takes it all in stride. Then:

" .....What makes you say that?" asks Ann.

"He wants to see us next weekend, Robert and me " answers Shirley.

"In Grasse?" asks Ann.

"Yes!"
"Oh?"

*"**Robert doesn't think that's why Dad wants to see us ?**"* added Shirley.

*"**Maybe he's right... I don't think Dad can make a decision like that so quickly... Mom is still so much a part of our lives .... What if Dad wanted to give us some bad news about his health?...Have you thought about that possibility?**"*

Ann asks a thousand and one questions, going from one (far-fetched) hypothesis to another (even more far-fetched), guessing, preparing (one never knows) the defense of her late mother against a father who would like to turn the page.

But after all, does she have the right to put her father under house arrest in her dream of preserving the memory of her late mother, against all odds?

Why can't her father continue his life as a man, in all simplicity, with a woman he feels comfortable with?

Isn't that his right?

Ann seems to forget that Americans are the champions (of all categories) of remarriage.

She also seems to ignore the old adage:
"The show must go on!"

"Life is the art of the possible," someone once said.

 So, if that's the case, why doesn't her father deserve another chance at happiness to live a happy and enchanting second life?

"Can you put Robert on?" asked Ann.

"OK! Bye!" replies Shirley.

"Hi Ann!"

"Hi Robert!"

"What's this about marriage?"

"I don't know, Shirley is sure of it. As far as I'm concerned, there's nothing to indicate

that. All I know is that Dad wants to see us. That's all I know. He told me exactly, bring your sister when I proposed to visit him in Grasse. And since then, it's been a mess. Shirley can't stand still. And I don't understand why she called you. Sorry!"

"So you're the one who asked for this appointment? And why on earth?"

"Dad called me this morning. Normally, he calls me on Monday for the weekly update. He wasn't his usual self. I sensed something unusual in the way he talked to me. As if he was preoccupied. So, not having the possibility to check, I asked him to go and visit him next weekend. And it was after I suggested the trip, that he asked me to bring Shirley. That's the whole story."

"I understand better....But when you say you detected something unusual, what exactly do you mean?"

"I'm not sure ... I can't explain it. ... I know my father. ... I can guess the slightest of his emotions ... But this morning, I did feel a certain discomfort in his way of addressing

me. I understood that there is something going on ... I am convinced that something important has happened."

"Robert, do you want me to come?"

"Do you think it's necessary?"

"Yes, I think it is! Don't you think Mom would have wanted this? She deserves to be fought for. Don't you think so? And it's our duty to do so. Don't you?"

"Agree with you, but, what if it's not?"

"Never mind, it will give us the opportunity to see each other all together in the south of France."

"Okay, I'll reserve you a seat on the next flight. Will Jerry come with you? Should I tell Dad?"

"No! Jerry will not be coming with me. Don't tell Dad. ... By the way, what's the status of dispersing Mom's things?"

"Nothing's done. I didn't have the courage."

93   Elvira PLYNN Greatness & Decadence

"And what does Dad say?"

"Nothing. ... I don't know if you know, he moved to another room upstairs. ... Probably not to live in this room where everything reminds him of mom. At least that's what I think."

"Ah? He left his room? With all his stuff?"

" No, I didn't know. Shirley didn't tell me."

" Oh that one!!!"

"I don't know, Ann. I don't know! Is it so important if he moved with or without his things?"

"Yes! Very important." she replied dryly.

"Ann! I understand you, but our mom is dead! We have to make up our minds....Dad loved and respected her. I think Mom was happy. That's the impression I always got from watching them live."

"Robert, you can't understand! What I mean is simple: if, he left his room with all his stuff, to me, that means he has turned

his back on his past, and permanently. He will never set foot in that room again.
This "past" that he wants to turn his back on, what is it, who do you think it is? Do you understand now what I mean?"

"Ann, yes, yes and yes! Who wouldn't understand? But at this point, we're not even sure what this invitation is about. It's not very healthy to lend this kind of intentions to our father, when all this started on a simple impression, felt this morning. ... So, please, let's not get excited! See you Thursday!"

"Okay! See you Thursday, Robert."

" Bye Take care."

15

After having hung up with Ann, Robert takes care of his sister's reservation.

In Grasse, it's the end of the day on Sunday.

Elvira invites Joseph to come and have a cup of jasmine tea and taste some vanilla financiers, bought from the best pastry in town.

She knows he loves them.

So why not use what he loves to bring him a little closer to her?

This time, Joseph didn't use a cab to get to the villa.

It was Elvira herself who took care of this mission, with happiness and delight.

On the way to the villa, Elvira takes advantage of each stop at the traffic lights to ask for a kiss.

Is Joseph fooled by the way she behaves like a woman madly in love, a woman to be cherished, a woman who would know how to wake up the sleeping ardors of a recent widower?

Nothing is certain. He seems to enjoy the moment without asking himself too many questions.

He did not lose sight of the fact that their meeting was the day before, and that even in the hypothesis of a "lightning" love at first sight, the behavior of his new friend and nevertheless recent lover, should not make him lose his footing and forget the essential: he does not know much about this woman who is the incarnate temptation.

When they arrive at the villa, they settle on the terrace on the garden side.

It is a very pleasant place of the villa in which the scents of a multitude of floral perfumes compete of diversity and power to impose themselves.

Elvira leaves him for a short while.

Joseph takes the opportunity to go for a walk in the alleys of the garden.

The flowers are really magnificent.

The tea is served.

The vanilla financiers also.

Joseph returns to settle down with his hostess.

The good mood of the day before seems to have disappeared.

Elvira feels a certain tension in him and is openly worried.

She does not understand.

What could have changed between this morning and this afternoon?

When she dropped him off, everything seemed normal.

What went wrong?

"Darling, what's wrong?" asks Elvira.

She wants to know for sure. She doesn't want to lose all the benefit of her investment. She has paid her own way, and she doesn't want to conclude that she did it all for nothing.

After a few moments of silence, Joseph decides to speak up.

"Well! Elvira, Through this unexpected

encounter, I've become convinced that, something has changed in my life. I felt happy and fulfilled at the same time. I also was surprised of the turn that took place in my life. My happiness would be complete if, I knew who I have in front of me. So, for the last time, may I know who you are ?"

Joseph does not sulk in his pleasure to have taken back the leadership in this relationship in which everything escaped him since the beginning.

Elvira smiles.

She takes Joseph's hand and puts it on her thighs. She asks him:

« *What do you want to know about me ?* »

« *My children will visit me soon. I would have liked to introduce you. But, I can't do it if I do not know who you are. Do you understand what I mean ?* »

« *Please Joseph, tell me exactly what you want to know. ... I, if I should to introduce you, I would simply say : may I introduce*

Joseph to you. …What could be simpler ? »

« *Ok ! … For example, what is your marital name ?* »

Elvira's face changes.

She drinks a cup of tea, then stands up and says:

"*WALKER! ... Next!*"

Joseph notices her annoyance.

"*Elvira, this not an inquisition. Relax! ... Just tell me something about you, allowing me to know you a bit more ....   But if you do not want to talk to me about your former life, it's ok. I fully understand your modesty. Maybe, you will open yourself to me later.*"

"*Thank you Joseph! Tell me darling when will your children come?*"

"*Next friday*".

"*You mean at the end of the next week?*"

"*Yes I do! Why?*"   asks Joseph.

"*Do you think they will accept an invitation to dinner here? ... It would be an opportunity to meet them. No ?*"

"*Certainly!*"

16

Second night at the villa.

The habits settle down.
Tiredness shows on the faces.
The features are drawn.
The nights are terribly agitated.
The nap becomes a vital emergency.

In spite of his distrust, Joseph feels alive

again. He feels invigorated by who knows what miracle.

 He is able to keep up with the pace imposed by his lover, he who never shone on this side in his previous life.

He answers as many times as it is necessary to the assaults of the one who is shaking up his existence. And he likes it. He feels flattered in his pride of male.

To each of her solicitations, he answers present. Sometimes, he anticipates the call. Um, who is the man in this case?

On the other hand, he discovers himself as an affectionate, tender and caring man, he who seems cold and distant, he who never knew how to be tender with his entourage.

This portrait that he makes of himself, does not correspond to him. He doesn't recognize himself in this idyllic picture that depicts him in his new life for two days.

What is most surprising for him, is that with

his advanced age, to which are added the side effects of his treatment against hypertension, everything should concur to limit his nocturnal prowess.

However, the opposite is true.

Is it the effect of the "novelty" or that of the cinnamon-flavored herbal tea Elvira prepares every night? That cup of herbal tea that waits for him on his bedside table, that potion that Elvira holds dear, making sure that it is consumed to the last drop before going to bed. (To be continued!)

On this Monday morning, Elvira does some shopping for Joseph: slippers, razor, shaving cream, toothbrush, toothpaste, comb, an assortment of white shirts, some spare underwear, ...

She returns to the villa, arms loaded with packages: the bare necessities as she says, for the comfort of her lover at home, and especially, so that this last one is not obliged any more to return to the property in the early morning.

Joseph observes all this with an amused air.

He knows that in a few weeks he must return home to Chantilly. Elvira knows it too. But even though she knows it, she still takes the liberty of putting together a trousseau for him.

On top of this trousseau, there is a set of keys to enter and move freely in the villa.

What does this mean? What is the reason why she is doing this?

Joseph, who is a brilliant mind, guesses the intentions of his new friend.

He begins to see the consequences of all this commotion around his modest person.

If he were to accept this trousseau, it would undoubtedly be a strong signal of encouragement to Elvira's efforts to capture his attention, a sign of hope for the future.

Paradoxically, he does not know what he wants.

To tell the truth, he doesn't feel ready to take the plunge, even though there's nothing stopping him from doing so.

But, how to put an end to this relationship born only two days ago?

How to deprive himself of all these attentions that make him the happiest and most important man on earth?

How can he abandon this outstanding cook who treats him to a thousand and one delights at the blessed hour of meals?

How to fight against this woman who wants to force her way in, and who wants him all to herself, even in the early morning?

How to stand up to her who wants to share everything with him and not only the moments of intimacy in the secret of the bedroom?

For the moment, he does not have the shadow of an answer to his questioning.

On the other hand, he is moved by all this solicitude.

He is impressed by all this devotion which certainly hides some intentions badly dissimulated by a woman who seems to love him with a crazy love and who wants to make him know it.

So, for the moment, he decides to let himself be won over by all this madness of the senses, until the arrival of the children. After that, he will decide.

In the space of two days, the unthinkable happened: Joseph began to dream of a life together.

But he doesn't show it.

He remains on his guard not to reveal himself, at least not for the moment.

17

In Kentucky, at the insistence of her fiancé, Ann finally explained the real reasons for her trip to France.

She didn't want to tell him what was going on, out of modesty, in order to preserve her father's private life, which should not be displayed in the public square.

Moreover, until then, she and her siblings are reduced to conjectures about the real intentions of their father.

They rely on an impression, even on an intuition, based on an invitation to go to the south of France.

That is all. That's all. Nothing more.

From this simple intuition, things went into overdrive.

Intuition proven or not, the moment of truth is not far: at the end of the week, everything will be clearer.

And so that her fiancé does not feel excluded from the family circle, she ended up telling him the whole affair.

Jerry finds exaggerated all this commotion for so little. But he is careful not to give reason to his future father-in-law in his possible desire to remake his life. He knows that such a position on his part, would put at evil his engagement with his sweet Ann whose attachment to her mother, is not a simple sight of spirit.

In accordance with the conclusions of the discussion she had with Robert, and to this end, Ann is frantically preparing her return to France.

She is leaving for three weeks.

She would like to take advantage of her stay to organize the dispersal of her mother's belongings, an organization that no one wants to take care of.

Three weeks might not be enough, especially if she also has to prepare for her father's remarriage!

"I'd rather break my leg!" she says to herself as she throws salt over her shoulders to ward off bad luck.

In the meantime, she placed urgent orders to stock up on pastries and other "made in Kentucky" victuals (including some of the ingredients to make the Hot Brown, the famous sandwich they all like so very much) for the family and for a few American friends living in France, in Paris or in the region.

Two days before her departure, Ann decided to go to Mammoth Cave National Park, near the giant sequoia.

She sits on the ground, leaning against the giant sequoia.

She remains silent.

She is there, just to remind her mother, that she will always be on her side, even if her father decides to start a new life.

She takes the opportunity to tell her that she is pregnant and to tell her, her big secret.

She is the first to know.

On a lighter note, she confides to her that she spends long hours in front of the mirror observing the roundness of her belly. But nothing is visible yet.
She is not in a hurry for it to show.

She doesn't know how to tell Jerry.

She aims at the good moment to announce to him what she has on the heart. She is waiting for him to finish this important project that he is currently working on, which is causing him a lot of stress.

She promises her to "regularize" the situation as soon as possible.

She hasn't forgotten how picky Barbara was about social conventions.

She promises her that everything will be fine, and that when her granddaughter or grandson is born, she will bring him/her to this place to say hello.

18

Thursday.

Paris, Roissy Charles de Gaulle Airport.

Ann PLYNN's plane has just landed.

Disembarkation of the passengers.

Robert and Shirley wait for their sister at the

exit.

Not too many two people to recover the excess of luggage.

Embraces, effusion of joy, happiness to be together again.

Direction Chantilly.

Arrival in Chantilly.

Big emotion : An absent one : Barbara.

Direction to Barbara's room.

Barbara's personal belongings remained in the state as in the last day.

Tears, more tears.

Great sadness, as if it were yesterday.

Ann returned to her room, unpacked and took a bath.

A light snack, then bedtime. She had to get

rid of the jet lag in order to be able to support the trip to the South of France the next day.

In Grasse, Joseph continues the good life at the villa with Elvira.

Cinnamon tea is prepared and served every night as usual.

The nights follow one another and are similar.

The naps are longer and longer.

A question of survival.

He had all the time necessary to take stock of the state of his feelings towards Elvira.

He never suspected that life can be as pleasant as the one he is living.

He questioned himself for a long time.

He came to the conclusion that he would not mind going a long way with her.

He does not regret the years spent with

Barbara, even if their relationship was only a mixture of puritanism and conventional rules, without much relief, without fantasy.

He does not regret either, the three beautiful children that Barbara gave him and who are his pride, even if his last one chose a way of life that the good old American society would condemn at that time.

What does it matter!

She is happy and that's the main thing.

Friday early afternoon.

Cannes Mandelieu airport.

The plane from Paris has just landed.

Disembarkation of the passengers.
At the exit, Joseph is waiting for his two children Robert and Shirley.

At his side, Elvira dressed in a strict azure blue suit, hair tied in a ponytail, wearing black patent pumps.

She is nervous. Joseph reassures her.

The door of the landing hall finally opens, letting escape a stream of passengers.

Suddenly, Joseph sees Ann accompanied by Robert and Shirley.

He is unsettled and wonders what is going on.

He doesn't have the blunder.

Ann is there, in front of him.

What does she come to do? Why is she there?

All three of them have closed faces.

They advance towards their father with a decisive step.
Shirley rushes in first, and throws herself into her father's arms.

"*Hello Dad!*"

As he hugs his daughter, Joseph keeps his eyes on Ann's face as she stares back at him.

He questions her with his eyes.

He wants to know why she is there.

He cannot explain the expression on his eldest daughter's face, which is not smiling.

He knows too well this expression which can announce a big storm.

He knows (having lived by her side for all these years), that his daughter can be particularly intractable and singularly lacking in flexibility.

Ann is a frontal person.

So, beware!

After kissing his daughter Shirley, Joseph, shakes hands with Robert and approaches his daughter Ann last.

"*What a nice surprise!*" he says slyly.

"*Hello Dad!*" she says curtly.

"*Hello Ann! How are you ? ... What happens ? ... Why are you here ? ... Something happened there ? ... Tell me ! How are you ? ... What happens ? ... Why are you here ? ... Did something happen there ? ... Tell me!*" he adds, his face worried and his voice quavering.

Joseph is not at the end of his surprise.

"*Who is this lady beside you?*" she asks sharply, staring at Elvira.

"*Is it true that you decided to replace mom?*" she adds in her stride.

Joseph is speechless. His throat is dry. His legs are flailing.

Before Joseph can even formulate an acceptable response to his daughter Ann's charge, in an unaccented English, Elvira enters the arena.

She stares Ann straight in the eye and in a dry voice:

"My name is Elvira Walker. ... I'm a friend of your Dad. ... I do not pretend to replace your mom. ... I accompanied your father to the airport to welcome you and to convey you. ... What else do you want to know about me?"

"As long as you are not Dad's girlfriend, it's ok!" Ann answers in a matter of seconds.

The situation turns sour.

Robert intervenes.

"Hello Elvira! Nice to meet you ! ... Thanks for coming to welcome us."

19

After this stormy and completely unexpected contact, everyone ends up getting into Elvira's vehicle.

She drives the 15 kilometers that separate Cannes from Grasse, in a minimum of time.

Once at the property, everyone gets out. Elvira continues her way to the villa, leaving

Joseph to face his children.

Will he be able to live up to the challenge and preserve their budding love?

The game is not won.

She must find a way to continue her project.

No matter what the means.

All her investment in time and in giving of herself cannot be written off.

In record time, she has captured Joseph's attention.
She knew how to transform him into an exceptional lover.
She was able to show him another side of life.
She managed to get him hooked on sex. And that's not the least of her merits, even if she used her little secret to do it.

What happened at the airport is indicative of what awaits her, if her intentions towards Joseph should materialize in the near future.

It allowed him to identify the "enemy" to be killed.

The "enemy" to be killed has a name: Ann!

She's not wasting any time, she thought.

At the same time, her best asset is Robert: more rounded, more diplomatic.

Shirley, it is the negligible quantity: nothing to fear from her. She will only make a mouthful.

Elvira has a very short time to find the right strategy before the end of the weekend, if she doesn't want Joseph to escape her permanently at the end of his stay in Grasse.

At the property, Joseph confronts his children.

This explanation that he dreads so much, is at the heart of this afternoon that started badly at the airport in Cannes.

He owes them an explanation concerning the

presence of Elvira at his side.

Then, methodically, very calmly, he begins to remind everyone of his loyalty to the memory of his deceased wife whom he loved with a sincere love.

For him, there is no question of taking a new wife to replace his late wife.

If he comes to this end, it is first of all, to fill a void and not to replace an absent person.

It's not an easy decision to make, he says.

He understands their concerns as much as he fears their anger.

He asks them in turn to understand him and to accept Elvira or any other person that he will have freely chosen at his side, to soften his second part of life.

Life is short, he tells them.

No reaction from the children.

He scans their faces, one after the other.

He wants to detect a sign, even the smallest one indicating him a beginning of approval.

No reaction.

Everyone stares into his eyes.

He feels overwhelmed.

He feels lost.

He is losing his children.

What can he do?

What other argument could tip the scales in his favor?

Nothing comes to mind.

A few moments later, to distract them and ease the pressure, he tells them of Elvira's intention to invite them to lunch at her house on Saturday.

Ann declines the invitation as dryly.

"*Rather die!*"   she says angrily.

"*Does she think, she can buy us by inviting us to eat? Who does she take us for?*" she adds.

Robert and Shirley remain silent and continue to stare into the eyes of this visibly distressed father.

Ann is not happy about what she considers to be a betrayal.

She doesn't know if she should blame her father or this woman who is trying to get her hands on him.

In any case, she refuses to accept the arrival of this stranger in the family, even if it means not setting foot in France again, as long as this union in the making is a reality.

20

In the villa, Elvira is boiling.

She browses her living room from one side to the other.

She frantically looks for what could allow her to reverse the situation in her favor.

She does not know how the situation at the property evolves.

She can't bear to be without news.

Have Ann and her siblings been able to bring their father to his senses?

Will she see Joseph again?

Has Joseph sided with his family?

Has she lost him forever?

She is on the verge of a nervous breakdown.

She decides to find out for sure.

She picks up the phone and calls Joseph.

No answer.

She redials the number.

Still no answer.

She goes crazy.

She grabs her purse and rushes out of the villa. She climbs into her car.

She starts in a hurry.

 Direction the property.

She drives like crazy.

The property is in sight.

She parks two blocks from the property.

She gets out of her car. She walks the last few meters.

There she is in front of the main entrance.

She rings the bell with a sharp knock. A second later, she rings again.

On the intercom, she hears Joseph's voice.

"**It's me!**" she says breathlessly.

"**I would like to see you. ... Please!**" she adds in a quavering voice.

A few moments later, the door opens.

Elvira sees in the doorway a man whose face shows the blow.

Joseph seems to have taken ten years in one go.

He is an unhappy man but happy to see a friendly face in the middle of the wreckage.

"Oh Joseph ... My poor darling ... It's entirely my fault about everthing that happens to you in this moment with your children. ... I feel guilty of engaging you into this story! ... Please forgive me darling. ... I do not know what I can do to change all this ... Joseph, if you want us to stop, just feel free to tell me, and I will let you go. " .

Elvira can't help but wipe away a tear. She seems very affected.

She plays her cards right.

It works!

Joseph can't stand to see her in tears.

He takes her in his arms to comfort her.

In his arms she feels so close and so far from happiness.

But, Joseph is at a crossroads.

The choice he has to make, one way or the other, does not satisfy him at all.

To choose his children at the expense of Elvira and to say goodbye to the evening cup of herbal tea and all that follows, or to stay with Elvira and let his children go, with a heavy heart.

Why is life so cruel? he thought.

And why should things be one way or the other, without ever leaving the possibility to act in all tranquility, in all freedom, without having to face the consequences of the choices that are made?

In this case, Joseph, of age and vaccinated,

should be able to direct his life without referring to anyone.

But instead, he puts himself in a position of subordination towards his children. This is beyond all comprehension.

Elvira could say to Joseph: choose me, and don't worry about the state of your children's souls, without incurring the wrath of Joseph who would see her selfishness in the middle of her face.

But in real life, nothing is logical.

This is an area in which God has got it all wrong, even if to get rid of the problem he has allowed men to invoke their free will.

Unless, in defence of this same God who created men, this is a pure invention of these men (divine creatures) to give themselves a good conscience, or else, to impose prohibitions and give themselves a bad conscience.

This could be similar to masochism.

Why do we want to earn what is given to us?

21

After a moment spent together in the garden of the property, Elvira goes back home a little more reassured, even if his brief interview with his lover does not guarantee the end of all their troubles.

She received fresh news, and that's the main thing. She does not ask more. At least for the moment. She doesn't dare hope for her lover tonight. But who knows?

For his part, Joseph returns to the boiling cauldron.

The battle is not over.

He would have preferred to enter the lion's den.

Ann's anger won't go away.

Robert tries to mediate.

It is almost an impossible task.

He knows his sister. He also knows that their father is in a very uncomfortable and humiliating situation.

That is why he must not lose face.

They must not make him lose face.

He doesn't want to, because Joseph PLYNN, before being this man sitting in the dock, is above all a respectable man.

He is a remarkable businessman.

He is a caring father who deserves respect.

He is an exceptional husband who loved with all his heart a woman named Barbara.

His position is clear: he does not want to be blinded by the duty of remembrance to which Ann seems to attach an exaggerated importance (from his point of view).

After all, why shouldn't this man have the right to do what he wants?

Why should this respectable family man have to suffer this ultimate grief by being humiliated by his children in front of the woman with whom he aspires to go on?

He is rather annoyed by the intransigent attitude of his sister, even if he understands her.

After all, Barbara, it is also his mother, and he does not make a whole dish of this history.

Without knowing it, Elvira is in the process

of winning the game.

Her master asset, a certain Robert PLYNN , takes cause and does for her.

She was not mistaken in considering him as her master asset.

Joseph, catches his breath.

A glass of whiskey in his hand, he settles in an armchair.

His glance betrays a deep anguish.

He measures the gravity of the moment.

He does not want to give up the essential.

He does not want to lose the possibility of resuming the course of his life.

He does not want to give up the expression of « LIFE » in him.

But how to translate all these concepts into actions?

22

.

At the villa, the doorbell rings.

Elvira rushes to the intercom.

On the screen of the surveillance camera, she sees Robert and his sister Ann.

Big surprise.

Her heart races.

She hesitates to open the gate.

Finally, she opens the gate.

After a quick look at her outfit and her hair, Elvira opens the door of the vestibule and appears on the small terrace lined with rosebushes in bloom.

At the same time, Robert and his sister enter the villa with a hesitant step.

She invites them to come inside.

Ann declines the invitation, preferring to stay in the garden.

Then, Elvira chooses to receive them on the terrace.

She invites them to settle down.

She offers them a drink.

Ann declines the offer.
Robert accepts a glass of orangeade.

Elvira complies. She disappears inside, and comes back with a tray on which there are three glasses and a carafe of orangeade.

She serves.

Despite Ann's refusal, she also fills the glass in front of her.

Robert decides to speak, in French. And in a very formal tone:

"I thank you for having accepted to receive us without an appointment.
We don't want our visit to Grasse to be a source of grief for our father. He has suffered enough since the death of our mother.
So, in agreement with my sister, I have taken the liberty of coming to see you to clarify two or three points, if you will."

"What do you want to know?" throws Elvira coldly.

Ann enters the fray.

"What are your intentions with regard to my father? " she says.

"What do you mean?" replies Elvira who wants to give herself time before answering this question.

"Do you intend to take advantage of my father's largesse? "

"Take advantage of your father's largesse?" astonishes Elvira.

"Yes!" insists Ann.

Elvira smiles and adds:

"Assuming your father and I, decide to get married, do you think it could be done without a marriage contract?
If you and your brother have come to insult me, then I won't hold you back."

Robert tries once again to calm the spirits.

"My sister just wants to know if what is going on between you and our father can be

called a serious relationship... And that you are not going to break his heart again. That's all."

"What is happening between your father and me, is a matter of what can happen between two consenting adults. ... On behalf of what, can you come to interfere in this story and want to rule everything? ... I do not care about the fortune of your father. ... This villa in which you come to lecture me, belongs to me. .... I'm not in the red, if that's what you think. On the contrary. I'm not an adventuress who runs after wealthy widowers.
... I have more than enough money to live out my days on this earth without ever going back to work. ... So if you want to prevent your father from seeing me again, do it and leave me alone! Otherwise, you are expected here tomorrow at noon to have lunch with your father.
One last point: I love your father deeply"
concluded Elvira, with a high voice.

© *Nathanaël AMAH , 2022   NATHAM Collection*

23

After the long tirade of Elvira, Robert and his sister leave the villa with the feeling of accomplished duty, even if it remains in their spirit, a reasonable doubt concerning the probity of the lover of their father.

Ann tries to bury the hatchet. She wants to make peace with her father after her outburst at the airport in Cannes.

Joseph has difficulty in accepting the excuses of his daughter.

He does not digest what happened.

He wonders how and by whom Ann could have been informed of this affair and why she felt obliged to make the trip from Kentucky.

He does not understand.

He does not believe in paranormal powers, like Barbara borrowing her daughter's body to come and make a scene.

He cannot deny this reality, even if he cannot explain it.

He questions Robert for a long time, but in vain.

Then, he decides to take his children to dinner in a restaurant in town.

He would have liked to have Elvira by his side, but the peace that reigns between him and his children still seems fragile.

The dinner goes well.

Joseph remained almost silent throughout the meal.

Even the latest news from Kentucky, reported and commented on by Ann, elicits no reaction from him.

He has become impervious to everything around him.

Joseph is wounded.

Like a wounded animal, he needs to hide in the depths of his cave, to lick his wound for a very long time before beginning a return to a normal life.

Moreover, a spring is broken.

This spring, which is called filial love and for which there is no after-sales service, is not made to fix the situation.

How can one blame his daughter Ann who wants to defend her mother on behalf of the duty of memory?

He tries to find the answer at the bottom of the glasses of white wine that have accumulated before him throughout the meal.

The meal finally ends. It is late.

They take a cab.

Robert whispers something in the driver's ear.

The cab starts.

A moment later, it stops in front of the villa.

Robert helps his father out of the cab and goes to ring the bell at the villa.

The light turns on on the small terrace.

The door opens.

Elvira, in a flowery negligee, appears in the doorway. She triggers the opening of the gate.

Robert accompanies his father in the

enclosure of the villa.

Elvira does not seem surprised.

She goes forward to welcome her Joseph.

Robert, very laconically:

"*See you tomorrow, 12:30!*"

"*Thank you Robert!*" answers Elvira.

Robert puts his hand on his father's shoulder, exerts a light pressure and leaves in the direction of the cab.

Elvira and Joseph enter the villa.

The light goes out on the small terrace.

The cab starts again.

Elvira runs a bath. She invites Joseph to take a bath.
Joseph complies.

Meanwhile, she is busy in the kitchen.

A few moments later, the cup of cinnamon tea is waiting for Joseph (as usual) on his bedside table.

The day that started badly, seems to end well.

Joseph, like an automaton, returns to the bedroom, swallows the contents of the cup and goes to bed.

Elvira, settles on the padded stool of her dressing table, and observes him for a long moment.

She savors her victory.

This is only the first step of her plan.

She did not forget the affront that Ann inflicted to her at the airport.

24

Saturday morning at the villa.

Gentle awakening.

The night was calm. Joseph needed to sleep to recover from all these nights without a real rest.

On her side, Elvira slept a good part of the night, while keeping a vigilant eye on her war catch.

The time of a shower, followed by a frugal breakfast and here they are occupied both to prepare the reception of the children of Joseph.

The morning will be short: the market, the delicatessen, the implementation in the kitchen, the setting in beauty of Elvira, ...

Everything is done in a hurry.

Elvira wants everything to be perfect.

She does not like to be late.

She has to be perfect even if Joseph is not to be taken anymore.

She makes it a point to take the whole family. She must not stop in such a good way.

The seduction must continue whatever the antagonisms.

Joseph has three children.

At the moment, she has only one of the three in her net. This catch is not the one she would have liked to have. But it's a good start, even if for her it's a grossly inadequate, almost disappointing result. She can do better. She knows it.

The hour advances.

In the kitchen, everything is under control.

Elvira does not speak. She is very concentrated.

Like a chef, she moves from one action to another with a disconcerting fluidity, (the moment being no longer for reflection), sometimes subcontracting her assistant cook for certain tasks, like stirring the spatula so that the contents of the pan do not stick.

A heavy responsibility indeed.

Joseph does it without flinching. He applies

himself.

He observes the mastery of this woman who impresses him more and more. She knows how to do everything.

He discovers the world of cooking. He puts a name to each action.

He discovers new smells.

Elvira is a recipe book on legs. She is able to quote from head, all that it is necessary to make such or such dish.

From time to time, she stops to check the progress of the cooking.

Joseph can see if everything is going well, just by looking at her face.

When Elvira brings the spoon dipped in the juices to her lips twice and raises her eyes to the sky, she makes sure that the alchemy of mixing flavors and aromas is being accomplished.

As a studious student, Joseph notes all these

details. One never knows, it may be useful to him one day soon.

But for the moment, he is unable to put a name on the dishes concocted by Elvira. He must wait to see the final stage (once the dishes are prepared) to get an idea.

12:45 p.m.

In the kitchen, everything seems to be under control.

Then, Elvira disappears in her room and reappears a few moments later.

From the cook in a white apron, professing the culinary art with talent, to the richly dressed creature who appeared in the middle of the living room, perfumed with expensive fragrances, her hair loose and flowing over her shoulders, Joseph barely recognizes Elvira, the woman for whom his heart now beats.

Between the conductor (with whom he has cooperated all morning at the market, in the delicatessen, in the kitchen), and the mistress, (the hostess, the supposed rival, a sparkling, luminous, radiant, magnificent, seductive creature), Joseph loses his bearings.

The metamorphosis is total.

The result exceeds all that he can imagine.

She is magnificent, a real enchantment for the eyes.

But this metamorphosis is only one means among others to achieve her ends.

Elvira has in mind the objective of the day: to rally the whole family of Joseph, including Ann, even if the deceased Barbara is in charge (as some will say).

1 p.m precisely.

One rings at the gate.

From the interior of the villa, Elvira activates the opening of the gate.

She goes out on the small terrace. Joseph follows her steps. She froze. She could not believe her eyes: only Robert and Shirley were present.

Despite everything, she kept smiling and went forward to welcome them.

She invites them in.

She asks Joseph to serve the aperitif and the petits fours.

"*I have to do a little last-minute shopping,*" she says as she leaves the house.

As soon as the door of the vestibule closed on Joseph and his two children, Elvira rushes outside, climbs into her vehicle and rushes towards the property.

She arrived in front of the gate of the property.

She waits a short moment in her vehicle, the time that her anger calms down, then, she gets down very calmly and approaches the gate.

She rings a sharp bell.

No answer.

She rings a second time.

A few seconds later, the door opens.

Ann appears in the doorway.

She triggers the opening of the gate.

Elvira penetrates in the enclosure of the property.

She advances towards Ann who does not move.

"*Hello Ann*".

"*Hello*".

"*I've come to pick you up*".

"*Are you joking?*"

"*No, I'm not kidding, Ann. ... I've come to*

pick you up. ... Go get changed. ... I'm waiting for you in the garden. Okay?"

Ann doesn't flinch.

She just stares at her. She can't believe her nerve. She begins to wonder about the real intentions of this person who wants to force her to follow her to the villa.

"Give me just one reason that could make me change my mind."

Without thinking, Elvira throws her:

"If you don't come for me, do something for your father."

"My father?"

"Yes, your father deserves the attention and affection of all his children, especially at this time."

Ann's curiosity is at an all-time high. But she doesn't want to show herself either interested or worried by the words of this woman whom she must distrust above all else and under all circumstances.

"*What do you mean?*"

"*Come, please!   Tomorrow I promise to tell you everything.*"

"*Do you take me for a fool?*"

"*No Ann! I promise to tell you everything tomorrow. But don't tell your father.*"

Now she's talking about disclosure.

Worry is slowly creeping up on her.

What does she have to reveal that is so important? What if her father really had a health problem that he was hiding from them? That could justify his behavior lately in deciding to get together with another woman.

"*OK! Wait for me!*"

Elvira, savors her victory. But her joy is of short duration, because at once, Ann goes out and comes back to the charge.

**" Is my father sick? I want an answer, NOW.
"**

**" I promised to reveal you all tomorrow.
Hurry up, they are waiting for us at the
villa."**

Ann stares at her for a moment, then goes back inside.

She reappears a few moments later.

During the time that Ann was preparing inside, Elvira thought about what she could tell her the next day about her father.

For the moment, she has managed to change her mind, but tomorrow, how can she keep a promise that is based on nothing?

In any case, she must find something, and quickly!

25

Seen from the outside, Elvira's insistence on gathering Joseph's entire family under her roof is surprising.

Is it the symbolism of this unity around Joseph that is important to her, or is it the catalytic effect of the presence of her children that could force him to inform his family very officially of his desire and decision to marry the woman he loves?

A third possible explanation: by acting in this way, she wants to create the ideal conditions to facilitate the advent of the couple she wants to form with Joseph.

The bet is risky.

Unless, her perfect knowledge of the psychology of his lover, allows her to envisage such an evolution during the reception which has begun at the villa.

The return of Elvira accompanied by Ann creates a shock.

Scalded by the insinuations of this mysterious woman who claims to have revelations, imagining the worst about his health, Ann rushes into her father's arms to embrace him with such fervor that the latter has difficulty explaining himself.

Robert is happy to see that tensions between his sister and father have finally eased, even if he does not understand how Elvira managed this feat.

Shirley observes all this with her usual detachment. She is more interested in the collection of knickknacks that she could use as inspiration for her art work.

Always on the lookout for the slightest opportunity to strike a blow, Elvira approaches Shirley and asks her to choose an object from her collection.

Shirley hesitates. She does not dare. Instinctively, her gaze goes to her sister who does not show (at first sight) any objection.

Then her choice is a Chinese doll of great value.

"*Are you sure I can?*" she asks.

Elvira gets a blow to the heart. This Chinese doll cost her a fortune at an auction. But she can't go back on her offer. A promise is a promise.

So very hypocritically:

*"**Yes Shirley! It is my pleasure to give it to you.**"*

*"**Thank you! Thank you so much!**"*

It's time to stop by for the lunch..

No seating plan.

Elvira settles down with authority between Joseph and Ann.

She proposes to form a chain by holding hands and asks Ann to recite grace.

She holds firmly Ann's hand and that of her lover.

She now wants to be the link between Joseph and his family.

Ann being the essential link, she needs this strong symbolic image of the eldest daughter giving her hand to ratify a situation in the making.

Elvira is not far from a symbolic image to strike the spirit and try to influence the destiny.

This is written in her DNA.

Moment of meditation.

Ann hesitates to launch this prayer which, by definition, serves to bless a meal shared by people present around a table, having the same disposition of heart and mind, living in perfect harmony.

She remembers the last blessings said by the deceased Barbara, when she was at the end of her life.

With a tight heart and a dull voice:

"Bless us Lord, as well as the food we are going to share. Amen!"

It was the shortest, the most neutral blessing she had ever said in her life.

Moreover, her hand clasped in Elvira's, in this

"enemy" hand that she is forced to touch, creates in her a feeling of rejection that she cannot control. It is beyond her strength. It is more than she can bear.

At the end of this very special blessing, Ann hurriedly removed her hand from Elvira's.
Very discreetly, she brings back her hand under the table, and she wipes it frantically on her skirt.

This operation of cleaning is not enough for her. She excuses herself, and to the general surprise, gets up and rushes in the bathroom.

Under the hot water, she starts again the cleaning of her hand.

Her dislike for this woman is real and tenacious.

Finally, she returns to her place, her hands reddened by the heat of tap water.

Lunch can finally begin.

The atmosphere is serene.

The dishes follow one another.

Joseph applies the instructions received in the morning. He takes an active part in the organization and the progress of the service.

But no statement from Joseph.

Elvira is getting impatient.

26

At the end of lunch, Elvira offers coffee on the large terrace lined with rosebushes in bloom.

Before joining his children on the terrace, Joseph helps to clear the table.

Meanwhile, Elvira is busy at the coffee

machine.

She prepares the tray on which she arranges the cups and the mignardises.

She seems preoccupied.

Joseph notices it.

"*What's wrong, darling?*" asks Joseph.

Elvira's anger explodes.

"*Joseph, what am I for you?*"

"*Why do you ask me this?*" replies Joseph.

"*I wonder what I mean to you. ... I have struggled to organize anything to welcome your family, but you, you pay no attention to me.... Not single emotional gesture during the lunch. ... Not a kiss. Nothing ! ... What do you believe your children think of me? ... The whore you fuck every night? ... When will you decide to talk to them about our relationship? ... As long as you don't tell them clearly, Ann will never be able to respect me. ... Do you understand what I mean? ... If you don't intend to talk to them, this is the last time you've set foot in my house."*

In the space of a few seconds, Joseph has just received in his face, an anthology of grievances held in the heart of his mistress.

It is the first time that he receives in a non dissimulated way, an injunction of this nature.

While arranging the plates and the glasses in the dishwasher, he cannot help hearing again these invectives asserted by Elvira a few moments earlier.

Should he consider these invectives as the expression of an ultimatum which translates a powerlessness or as the echo of the last requirement before the capitulation?

Capitulation ?

Does Elvira have any choice but to maintain the status quo by continuing to serve the cup of herbal tea and shelter their guilty love in the secrecy of her bedroom, waiting for better days?

Or as a last resort, admit defeat and retreat with what remains of the honor she has sacrificed until this very moment?

He wonders.

It is far from the time when the cup of herbal tea is served with benevolence before the evening cuddle.

In any case, it is not in his nature to bend to the injunctions of anyone.

For now, lunch must end on a high note.

"*I fully understand what you mean,*" replies Joseph.

"*So, if you understand, it's time to talk to them!!!*" she said in a dry tone

On this, Elvira fills the cups and asks Joseph to carry the tray on the terrace.

She follows him with her "natural" smile.

All is well!

Gathering around the garden table.

Elvira suggests to Joseph that he serve.

Joseph gets up.

Still worried about her father's supposed state of health, Ann forces him to sit down again, and takes charge of serving the coffee.

Elvira serves the mignardises.

27

At the end of the service, Joseph asks to speak.

"May I have your attention please?"

Elvira flashes her best smile.

"First of all, I would like to thank Elvira for organizing this delicious lunch. Over time,

she became more than a friend to me. What I mean, from now on, I want you to consider her as part of my life."

Every word spoken is weighed. Every word heard is heavy with meaning.

But Elvira is still hungry.

Joseph has not announced their engagement.

She doesn't care that she is the most important person in his life. She doesn't care about phrases that don't mean anything at this stage of their relationship.

What she wants is a statement that will make her the future Mrs. Elvira PLYNN.

Joseph seems not to understand.

She feels the mustard rising in her nose.

"*I must consider myself as a part of your life? It's what I need to understand ? Could you please explain to your children what you mean? Is that what I need to understand? Could you please explain to your children what you mean?*" she asks.

"*Elvira, what do you want me to explain?*" asks Joseph.

Elvira is exasperated by this question, which she finds silly.

"*The reality of the situation. It would be a good start to tell them that you and me, we share more than an ordinary friendship. No?*" she says in a peremptory tone.

Joseph doesn't dare look at her in the face.

"*Dad, what does she mean?*" asks Ann, coming to the rescue of her father, who seems to be in trouble.

"*... we enjoy being together.*" replies Joseph.

"*So what? What should we understand?*" asks Ann.

"*... We love each other.*" replies Elvira coldly.

"*Is that true Daddy?*" worries Ann.

And before Joseph has time to answer, Elvira makes her point:

"*...We love each other and we could decide to join our loneliness.*"

This last intervention of Elvira finishes to plummet definitively the cordial atmosphere hardly created by Joseph and his family.
Each one put a little of the good will there for the success of this lunch.

"*And when is the wedding?*" Ann ironically asks.

This question, which is pure irony, finds a certain echo in Elvira.

She is so anchored in this idea of officialization of their relation, that all questions touching this domain, deserve a direct and immediate answer.

"*As soon as possible!*" she replies.

Ann bursts out laughing.

"*Are you joking?*"   she retorts.

"*I seem to be joking?*"   replies Elvira almost angrily.

"*And you Dad, you say nothing? ... It seems that you are about to get married. That's true ?* " asks Ann her father, who seems to be somewhere else and is unaware of what is going on around him.

"*To get married, you have to be two. No?*" adds Ann.

Elvira shrugs her shoulders. Then in an almost threatening tone:

"*What is your problem?*"

"*My problem ? ... You dare to ask me ? I do not want to leave my poor father helpless with a stranger. Is that enough of a reason?*" replies Ann.

Elvira bursts out laughing.

*"**Me, a stranger? ... OK Ann, pick up your father, and get out of my house!**"* she orders.

With these good words, Elvira pretends to retreat inside the villa.

Suddenly, before she crosses the threshold of the door, very calmly, Joseph asks her to come back and sit down.

She does not need to be asked, and returns at once to sit beside her lover.

It was time to react.

She blames him for leaving her to fight on her own against this calamity named Ann.

She loses nothing to wait. Word of Elvira.

For the moment, she waits for the continuation of the intervention of Joseph.

28

Joseph followed with a certain sadness, the stormy and bellicose exchanges between his daughter and his mistress.

Since the beginning of his relationship with Elvira, Joseph navigates between two contradictory feelings.

On the one hand, his fidelity to the memory

of his wife Barbara who gave him and left him three beautiful children who make him proud, on the other hand, his ardent desire to fill his loneliness at the sides of Elvira who does not spare her efforts to seduce him by allowing him to have another vision of the life, even if, he does not know much about her.

Joseph knows that on either side, his choice would do irreversible damage.

The challenge is to try to bring the two sides of the abyss in which he finds himself, closer together.

In the commercial field, it would have been enough for him to find the right financial arguments to make each of them give up their most extravagant demands.

But in this case, between his daughter who wants to preserve the memory of her deceased mother and his mistress who already sees herself with a ring on her finger, how to do it?

Joseph scrutinized his son Robert's face (which had remained silent until that moment), but he could not detect the slightest desire on the part of his son to come to his rescue by finding the right words to ease the tensions between these two women.

Robert has learned everything from his father. This father, of whom he is proud and whom he respects above all else, must once again show him that he is and remains the great, the unique, the impressive, the respected, the fearsome JOSEPH   PLYNN!

Robert is not worried.

The silence observed by his father during the confrontation between these two women dear to his heart, is by no means a sign of weakness, nor a way of showing his powerlessness to solve the problem (opposing these two women), which seems insoluble.

Joseph PLYNN never capitulates.

He knows that from this silence, a flash of brilliance can emerge that will allow him to win the game, by putting in agreement these two women to whom he is particularly attached.

Then, against all odds, he gets up, grabs two garden chairs that he installs away from the group, and asks his daughter to join him.

Ann complies.

They sit facing each other.

"*Ann,*" he says.

"*Yes Dad!*" replies Ann.

"*You know me. You know who I am. You know how strong my love for your mother was.*"

"*Yes, I do,*" replied Ann.

"*So please, tell me what is wrong,*" asks Joseph.

Ann stares into her father's eyes for a moment, then:

"Dad, what do you know about this woman, except that, she claims to be Elvira Walker ? Do you know her family ? ... I know you well enough. And as a wise man, I know that you will never do business with a person about whom you ignore everything. So Dad, tell me please, how can you entrust your life to a woman you ignore everything ? Please tell me!"

Joseph grabs both of his daughter's hands, squeezes them tightly and kisses them.

What could he say to someone who makes sense and asks common sense questions?

"Ann, your questioning is full of common sense. I expect no less from you. You are an adult person. Is it necessary to explain to you, why suddenly our heart beats harder in front of a person we do not know or hardly know ? That's right I know almost nothing about her. But, my heart and all my being ask me to go to her. Can you understand that?"

"Daddy, is that really what you want?" asks

Ann.

*"**Yes Ann, that will be enough for my happiness.**"* replied Joseph.

*"**One more thing Dad: Promise me to take care of yourself. For my part, I'll investigate her when I'll be back to the USA.**"* adds Ann resignedly.

After that, the two get up and rejoin the group.
Joseph proposes to uncork a bottle of champagne to celebrate the engagement.

Elvira does not get prayed.

29

The engagement is celebrated in an unusual atmosphere.

On one side of the table, Joseph's children, on the other, Elvira and her new fiancé.

No joy on the faces. In the hearts, it is another story.

Now, it remains to find a date for the wedding.

Ann will not be able to attend the wedding. The company's business in Kentucky will not allow her to make a return trip to France anytime soon.

However, she would be able to see her father again if Elvira agreed that part of their wedding trip could be spent in Kentucky.

This will not be the case: Elvira refuses to set foot in the United States again.

The main reason: she doesn't want to.

She wants to discover another part of this wide world as she says.

Australia for example, a country for which she discovered a sudden passion for a person who hates long plane rides.

Is there an extradition agreement between Australia and the United States?

That's what Joseph overheard when he overheard a phone conversation between his fiancée and a mysterious caller.

A strange question indeed for an honest, loving, devoted fiancée who owns a villa in France and intends to marry in France.

Why such a question?

Joseph tries to find out a little more, but in vain.

He reassures himself by thinking of his daughter's promise to investigate her. He hopes that he will know a little more about her past life very soon, preferably before the celebration of the wedding.

Ann returned to Kentucky a few weeks later.

Her main concern: how to tell her fiancé Jerry that she is pregnant and that the child in her belly is not his?

Indeed, this child cannot arrive at a worse time than this period during which, she lives a deep upheaval since her stay in France.

She remembers perfectly this stay in New York, during which she crossed paths with this representative from Augusta in the state of Maine, who had come to attend the annual convention of cereal producers.

Originally from Canada, Joshua's family moved from New Brunswick to Maine in the 1940's where they prospered in the agri-business.

Joshua knows Ann through their respective businesses without ever having seen her in real life.

They talk on the phone often. They like each other. There is a real complicity between them.

Joshua knows that Ann has a fiancé and that the wedding will take place very soon.

But that doesn't stop their first meeting on the opening day of the grain convention from overshadowing everything else.

The attraction of one to the other is a reality.

A real love at first sight. They do not leave each other of the eyes. They hate the organizer who placed them on the opposite side of the room.

The day passed without a hitch.

At the podium, the different cereal producers come to compare their production methods. Each one boasts of having the best yield per hectare.

Ann PLYNN takes the floor for the first time.

A little intimidated at the beginning, she begins her speech by paying a tribute to her grandfather John PLYNN, after having transmitted the greetings of her father Joseph PLYNN, retained in France.

With method and conciseness, Ann demonstrates (with figures to support) the need to finance research centers for the development of new methods of cultivation: adaptation of seeds to the nature of the soil, according to the regions and the climate. This will allow (she says with some confidence) to improve yields and thus guarantee better profits per hectare.

Ann PLYNN's recommendations caused a sensation and aroused general enthusiasm. Joshua broke all records in terms of applause.

During the closing dinner, the two friends get closer and share the same table.

Joshua tries everything to get Ann PLYNN to agree to come up to his suite for a last drink.

Ann softly resists this invitation, then finally, agrees to accompany Joshua to the thirty-second floor of this hotel which offers a breathtaking view of the city.

The elevator starts and releases its passengers floor after floor.

Joshua and Ann are lurking at the bottom of the elevator.

Joshua is getting impatient.

Ann still has time to give up.

Her legs no longer carry her.

Nineteenth floor.

Will she get off and take another elevator in descent mode?

Next stop: the twenty-sixth.

After that, direct ascent to the thirty-second floor.

Ann still doesn't decide to go down.

After all, what does she risk?

A drink and then what?

What's wrong with accepting a drink from her friend Joshua?

She tries to reassure herself. She has never known such a feeling of having to resist a temptation.

Her life of well-ordered young girl, under the leadership of Barbara, did not prepare her to face such a situation, since, in any case, that should not be done. It is not correct to accompany a stranger in his room, even for a last drink.

Thirty-second floor.

The elevator door opens.

Joshua gets out first.

Anne seems to hesitate.

Joshua stands between the two doors to prevent them from closing. He holds out his hand to her.

Ann grabs his hand.

Joshua pulls her out of the elevator.

Ann shakes all over.

Joshua holds her hand firmly in his, and

heads for his suite.

Ann follows.

Door 32018.

Joshua takes out his pass and opens the door.

He invites Ann to enter first.

Ann does so.

Joshua enters in his turn.

Suddenly, against all odds, very calmly, Ann says:

"***Let's do it right away, like that, we don't think about it anymore. Yes?***"

Joshua couldn't believe his ears. He doesn't know what to say. Is this a joke to throw him off balance?

Joshua is petrified. He can't imagine for a moment that this girl from a good family could make such a proposal. Usually, he is the one in charge. He is the one who seduces. He is the one who finally overcomes the most fierce resistance. He is the one who triumphs.

Ann joins the gesture to the word, and begins to undress.

She is now completely naked.
She moves towards the bed.

Joshua remains perplexed, but ends up joining her.

30

The investigation carried out by Ann about her future stepmother, gives no result.

Elvira Walker does not appear anywhere : neither in the civil status, nor in the files of the prosecutor's office, nor in the newspapers specialized in the facts.

It is as if Elvira Walker had never set foot in the United States.

The Elvira Walker mystery remains.

By informing her father of the result of her investigation, Ann cannot help trying once again to make him give up his project of marriage.

But it is difficult to dissuade him from it. The banns are published and the wedding is in one week.

It will not be a big ceremony. Just a visit to the town hall with some friends, and then a reception in a big hotel in Cannes.

The children are invited.

Elvira has no desire to go and live in Chantilly and form a threesome with Barbara's ghost.

Therefore, she wants to buy an apartment in the Madeleine district of Paris.

A very small apartment of one hundred and fifty square meters. Something modest. Nothing too extravagant. (Translate!)

Joseph asks Robert to take care of the financing.

Robert takes the opportunity to ask the family notary to draw up a codicil to the marriage contract.

Upon learning this at the time of the signing of the documents, Elvira went into a rage, threatening to break off the engagement and renounce the marriage if there was not a minimum of trust between them and if Joseph could not determine his own way of life without constantly referring to his children.

During this period, during which the signing of the marriage contract was suspended, Joseph was no longer allowed to have a cup of herbal tea or evening sex sessions behind the closed bedroom door.

Total sex strike, voted by her and renewable night after night.

Joseph can no longer bear the atmosphere created by the establishment of this marriage contract restricting the prerogatives of the future wife.

Elvira knows that " PLYNN " is first of all a very respected family name. It is a registered trademark. It is a flourishing family business. It's huge capital in several businesses across the United States.

She has conducted her own investigation since the scallop nuts episode.

She knows exactly how much Joseph weighs and her plan takes all of these details into account.

Robert must not be the thorn in her side.

She had made him her ally, but she is beginning to regret it.

She has invested time and money. She doesn't want to give up so close to her goal.

In a very heated discussion with his son, Joseph manages to get him to drop the marriage contract.

Robert agrees to stop demanding the marriage contract, but hurries to contact the notary to find the ultimate solution to protect the family just in case.

Joseph announces the good news to his fiancée.

End of the strike.

The cup of herbal tea reappears.
The naughty nighties and the nightly treats too.

The endless sessions are back on the agenda.

Life returns to normal.

Joseph is happy.

31

The wedding: D-day.

At the town hall of Grasse, the mayor of the town celebrates this wedding which is like no other.

Have we ever seen the bride's family members absent from a wedding celebration?

In the memory of a registrar, this has never

been seen.

Zero percent of presence on Elvira's side.

What a surprise for the audience who asks themselves a thousand and one questions.

To Joseph, she claims to have been annoyed to death with her family.

A sordid story of inheritance between her sister and her brother.

Her parents having died, there is no one left to represent her family at her wedding: neither cousins, nor nephews nor nieces, the latter having taken up their parents' cause.

For her, the situation is extremely clear.

She does not understand why this is a source of concern for the PLYNNs who, as everyone knows, are united in a large, wealthy and supportive family.
On Joseph's side, Robert and Shirley are present at the ceremony.

Some American friends made the trip from Paris. Fortunately!

Otherwise, the audience would have been sparse in this large wedding hall of the town hall.

The morning of the wedding, Joseph received a telegram from the USA, signed Ann PLYNN :

"Good luck!"

A laconic message that reflects Ann's state of mind, who prefers to spend this day in Mammoth Cave National Park, not far from the giant sequoia.

Over time, Ann has calmed down but not appeased.

The fate of her father continues to be a source of concern for her, even though she has broken off her engagement with Jerry and her pregnancy continues without Joshua's knowledge.
She regularly checks on her father with her

brother Robert.

She learns, among other things, the story of the quarrel (caused by the marriage contract), which almost caused the marriage to fail, and which reinforces her idea that caution must always be exercised.

Therefore, on her side, (based on the American legislation in force and insofar as the family's assets are of American origin), certain arrangements are made from the United States with the family's lawyers to limit the damage just in case.

On the other hand, since her failure at the end of her investigation on her possible future stepmother, a question does not cease to torment Ann:

Who is hiding behind Elvira Walker ?

And if " Elvira WALKER " was an assumed name ?

It's so easy to impersonate someone else.

A few thousand dollars and it's done. No need to see or hear about it!

It's a new lead to dig, but the outcome is just as uncertain unless, tongues are loosened following a generous reward offer.

She asks her brother to take advantage of the wedding to take pictures so as not to arouse her suspicions.

To be continued.

At the end of the wedding celebration, when the mayor congratulates the couple while giving them the family booklet, Elvira extends her hand and takes back the precious booklet.

Feverishly and in front of the stunned mayor, she opens the main page, checks the veracity of the inscription of her name with all the legal mentions conferring her the status of wife of Joseph PLYNN.

Now she is sure that she is Elvira PLYNN!

This is step number two of her plan.

Elvira WALKER is dead, long live to Elvira PLYNN.

32

Departure of the procession formed by the cars placed at the disposal of the guests.

Direction Cannes.

Hotel MARTINEZ.

Elvira PLYNN, on the arm of Joseph PLYNN makes her entrance in the reception room.

Acclamations.

For Elvira, it is the cherry on the cake.

At the request of Robert, Shirley takes pictures, many pictures for Ann.

Shirley is not aware of the plan to find out who is behind Elvira Walker and thus, to unmask her.

Magnificent reception.

Some speeches.

Musical entertainment.

Everything seems perfect, but Elvira is bored.

She wants to be somewhere else.

A few moments later, she asks her husband to leave.

The couple takes their leave.

Direction: the bridal suite.

Usually, before the big day, the mother of the bride or, failing that, the inseparable friend of the heart, gives to the young bride the very last recommendations on the course of the wedding night.

For the young bride, who is supposed to know nothing about life, the wedding night is anything but a fairy tale.

But, in her new clothes of real young bride, Elvira PLYNN does not intend to sacrifice to the tradition.

Besides, she has neither mother, nor best friend to advise her. She is all alone to face this wedding night and her intentions are of another order.

As soon as the door of the suite closes, Elvira get out of her bag, a three-page document folded in four, to be signed without delay by her new husband.

Joseph, whose brain is foggy from the alcohol ingested during the evening, does not understand much of what his wife commands him to do.

He must initial each page of this mysterious document, and then sign the last page.

That's all, then he can sleep.

After this mock wedding night, Joseph emerges the next day, exactly around 11:30 am.

He does not remember anything.

When he wakes up, he finds a note from his wife on the pedestal table, informing him of her absence for an urgent errand.

When he returned from the shower, Joseph found his wife sitting on the sofa, waiting for him to go to lunch.

"*Where were you?*" asks Joseph.

"*Honey, I went on an errand in town.*" replies Elvira.

Then she opens her bag, takes out a package

and gives it to Joseph, saying:

"Honey, here is your wedding present. ... It is the least I can do to thank you for the support and consideration you have given me by accepting that our relationship becomes a fairy tale. ... My husband, how I love you! Please, never doubt my feelings for you. OK? "

Joseph frees his hands, receives the package, opens it and discovers a solid gold watch.

He turns it over. He discovers an engraved inscription:

« *To my husband, with all my love* »

He is surprised, but, aren't we in Cannes?

He approaches. He takes her in his arms. He kisses her for a long time.

She lets herself do it.

She is in love.

Very in love.

She is cuddly.

She abandons herself.

She drags him towards the bed.

She wants Joseph to make love to her, right now.

33

Return to Grasse at the end of the day.

Life resumed its course at the villa.

One thing leading to another, Elvira was given a monthly allowance to cover her small expenses.

This allowance, equivalent to a senior executive's salary, fixed by Robert in agreement with his father, seems (for the moment) to suit her.

Another account is used for household expenses and the maintenance of the villa, which suddenly needs a complete restoration.

Officially, the purpose of this restoration is to make it a little more comfortable and functional to welcome Joseph and his family.

The company chosen to carry out the restoration work is a company from Marseilles, warmly recommended by an old acquaintance.

While waiting for the restoration to be completed, Elvira proposes to move back to Paris.

They will be able to live in the apartment located in the Madeleine district and not in Chantilly.

She will be able to come down to Grasse from time to time to supervise the work and follow the progress of the restoration in real time.

This return to Paris allowed Joseph to be more in touch with Robert who had taken on more responsibilities during his father's absence in the south of France.

He organizes conference calls with the United States.

Ann is delighted to be working with her father again.

With the photos of the wedding, the research on Elvira Walker starts again.

Joseph is unaware of this new initiative.

Ann does not know in what state of mind her father is at this moment, several weeks after his marriage.

Would he still agree to diligently start a new investigation on his wife?

They don't dare ask him.

In any case, Robert and his sister's ambition

is to protect their father against all odds. They don't want their father to be under the influence of this woman they don't know anything about and who doesn't inspire confidence in them.

Since she is working with her father again, Ann takes pleasure in confiding in him.

Joseph learns that he will soon be a grandfather. But the father of this child who will be born, will not be Jerry. Indeed, Jerry broke the engagement for reasons that Ann does not want to explain to him for the moment.

Joseph is sad to learn that. He thinks of Barbara who appreciated Jerry a lot.

Since their installation in the apartment, Elvira returned twice to Grasse at the request of the old friend.

Her absences last between three and five days.

Sometimes the old friend drives her back to

Paris, without daring to go up to the apartment.

One day, a little more motivated than the other times, he came to the apartment to talk with Joseph.

Joseph recommended that he make an appointment with his son Robert.

On the agreed day, Robert saw a disreputable person arrive who threatened to stop the work if he did not agree to an immediate payment of one hundred thousand euros.

However, at the beginning of the work, a provision of two hundred thousand euros was transferred to Elvira's account.

The supposed head of the works claims not to have received anything to date.

Robert picks up the phone and informs his father of the situation.

Joseph asks his wife for an explanation.

Elvira raises her arms to the sky, swearing to God that everything has been done in time and that the foreman has been paid.

Who is to be believed?

Robert demands that his stepmother provide proof that the advance payments have been made.

Impossible: with the work, some documents have been moved and she cannot get her hands on the accounting documents Robert is asking for.

Moreover, everything is in Grasse and obviously, as she is in Paris at the moment, she cannot do anything.

Therefore, it was totally impossible to satisfy Robert's demands.

She urged her husband to settle this matter, which was tiring her unnecessarily.

Moreover, she starts to feel a violent migraine.

A headache that could deprive him of his evening cup of herbal tea, a tea that his children do not know exists until now.

Robert sees red. He gets angry.

He wants to talk to his father in private, without delay.

In the meantime, the supposed head of the works is installed in a small hotel in the Saint-Lazare district.
He must return to Grasse the next day to see the workers and pay them.

A stormy discussion between Robert and his father.

Robert suggests to suspend all payments to Elvira, until the situation has been clarified.

Joseph opposes this.

Robert suggests to give up the restoration of the villa which does not belong to them.

Joseph objects: a commitment is a commitment, he reminds him.

Faced with his son's inflexible attitude, Joseph decides to pay the hundred thousand euros claimed by the supposed head of the works from his own money.

Immediately, Elvira's headache disappeared as if by magic.

The supposed foreman can travel again the next day, as planned.
Robert begins to perceive the strategy put in place by his stepmother.

Siphoning off as much as she can of the family's finances, with or without the complicity of a third party.

As the situation in the USA is under control, he considers it appropriate to take similar measures in France to protect the family.

All the bills must be sent to him, and payments will no longer be made through Elvira.

Robert is not happy to see his father being robbed of one hundred thousand euros without him being able to intervene.

Ann is immediately informed of the situation.

She is horrified by the turn that takes the marital life of her father.

She blames herself for having been right all along, and for having failed to prevent this marriage.

She feels guilty, and her hatred for Elvira is increased tenfold.

Ann suggests to her brother to carry out a discrete investigation on the supposed head of the works, and if possible, to deposit complaint for swindle.

34

Elvira stubbornly refuses to set foot on the family property.

The reasons for this refusal have not changed.

Consequently, Joseph goes alone to Chantilly

for the day organized in memory of Barbara, a day which must end with the dispersion of Barbara's personal belongings in the presence of some selected charities, in charge of collecting the proceeds of the sale of the valuable pieces auctioned in the beginning of the afternoon in the property.

Ann regrets not being able to participate physically in this day, but is delighted with this initiative which, according to her, puts an end to the mourning period.

The end of the mourning period will not prevent the memory of Barbara to remain forever engraved in their hearts.

Ann manages to win some auctions, allowing her to keep most of her late mother's precious jewelry for herself and her sister Shirley.

Upon his return to the apartment, Joseph learns that Elvira intends to make another trip to Grasse.

The official reason:

an important decision to be made regarding

the choice of a material to replace another one that no longer suits her.

Joseph offers to accompany her to help her make her choice.

He wants to participate in some way in the restoration of this villa, even though he does not actually own it.

Elvira does not want to sell him the villa, which she claims has great sentimental value for her.

However, he finances the entire restoration work. This should, in principle, give him the privilege of imposing his choices which will allow him to feel a little more at home, when the work is finished.

Nothing more logical indeed.

But Elvira doesn't see it that way. She categorically refuses to let her husband accompany her on her inspection tour.

The alleged reason: the dust generated by

the work would be incompatible with his health.

Health condition?

Is Joseph ill?

First news.

Joseph is troubled.

He had never spoken to her about his health.

It is true that he has high blood pressure and asthma, but both are under control.

On the other hand, there has never been the slightest visual, embarrassing manifestation of these two conditions in her presence.

So how can she know?

By reflecting, he remembers resorting to his aerosol after a coitus that went beyond the limit of what could be considered reasonable.

He had had trouble catching his breath. So, very discreetly, he had used his aerosol to relieve his bronchial tubes.

For the first time, in his mind, there was no longer any doubt. Joseph no longer saw his wife with the eyes of a loving and confident "newlywed".

So, after Elvira's departure, Joseph asks Robert to go to Grasse to try to see what is going on there (to the great surprise of the latter, who finally sees his father's point of view join his own concerning Elvira).

« *It's necessary for man, to be happy, that he should move forward on prudence, and enlightened by reason.*» he adds.

Robert is reassured.

Joseph is back with his family.

His reasoning, which had been reduced to privileging feelings, to considering mystery as an integral part of the feeling of love, allows him once again to see clearly in his relationship with his wife.

His momentary blindness before his marriage

is now a distant memory.

But for Elvira to continue to believe that all the cards are in her hands, he has to keep his eyes half closed.

His critical mind, (his safety valve), is back in action.

The dreaded businessman named Joseph PLYNN is back.

He immediately calls Ann to keep her informed.

Ann recommends to him to observe the greatest prudence.

Elvira could be dangerous if she feels cornered.

Before leaving his father's apartment, Robert goes to the kitchen. He needs a cup of coffee.

He looks for the coffee packet. He finds packets containing bags of plants to prepare various infusions: digestion, sleep, ...

But, he notices at the bottom, But, he notices at the bottom, a packet on which he can see inscriptions in Cyrillic characters. on which he can see inscriptions in Cyrillic characters.

Robert does not know how to read Russian.

He brings the package to the living room and shows it to his father.

Joseph does not read Russian either, so he does not know what it is about.

He does not pay any more attention to the package of herbal sachets.

He knows, however, that he has been entitled to a cup of herbal tea every night since he started dating Elvira.

Robert is surprised to learn this.

Herbal tea for what? he asks.

So he takes a sachet from the box, puts it in his pocket and puts the packet back in its place.

He prepares his cup of coffee, spends a moment with his father and takes his leave.

On arriving in Chantilly, Robert stops at the pharmacist's and asks him to perform a toxicological analysis of the contents of the sachet.

Then he goes home.

35

It has been two days since Elvira returned to her villa in Grasse.

Robert refines his strategy to unmask his stepmother.

He summons a private detective and assigns him the delicate mission of investigating Elvira.

Elvira PLYNN Greatness & Decadence

One day of investigation was enough to obtain the information expected by the client.

In the memory of a detective, an investigation has never been so facilitated by the incredibly disrespectful and casual behavior of the two protagonists in an adultery case.

The conclusions of the private detective are without appeal.

Elvira and the supposed head of the works (Andreil of his first name and Russian origin), are lovers.

It is an open relationship. They know that nobody in the entourage of Joseph PLYNN threatens their peace.

The photos reported by the detective are unequivocal.

It is not a question of a parenthesis in her young married life, but well and truly of the continuity of a former relationship.

The photos attest to this.

Indeed, Andrei and Elvira were married in another life, when they were both living in the USA.

In New York where Andrei had a Russian bar.

Elvira was in charge of the annex of the bar, pompously renamed :

"The VOLGA grocery store".

A delicatessen where the whole Russian community would come and leave a fortune day after day.

Once a month, Andrei made the trip to Moscow for supplies.

During his absence, Elvira took over the management of the two establishments and ruled over them with all the authority of a formidable businesswoman.

Elvira had everything: husband, money, consideration.

But her desire was elsewhere.

A real obsession.

She wanted to change her name.

To have a good American name.

For what purpose?

To blend in with American society. This is hardly possible with a name of Russian origin.

Her resolution was clear: to start over from scratch, to live her American dream in broad daylight and not from the back of a grocery store.

So, without telling her husband, and in exchange for several thousand dollars, Elvira managed to obtain papers in the name of Elvira Walker.

Elvira AZAROV gives way to Elvira WALKER.

All this without Andrei's knowledge.

New identity, new aspirations.

Elvira likes the good life. Nothing can be too good or too expensive for her. She wants to live another life. She has other ambitions.

The VOLGA grocery store has become too small for her dreams of expansion and Andrei, a major obstacle to her new projects. Because Andrei, who inherited the business from his father, does not want to give up the family property.

They discussed it for many nights, in vain.

So, tired of fighting, she decided to end it all.

A solution must be found.

She wrote an anonymous letter in which she denounced Andrei AZAROV for tax fraud.

Convoy of police cars, arrest, trial, incarceration.

Her numerous expressions of love for her husband, her tears, her despair, everything is done to cover her tracks and avoid being suspected by Andrei who is rotting in prison.

The two establishments are closed *de facto*. The bank accounts are seized.

The proceeds from the sale of the Russian bar and the VOLGA grocery store were used to pay for the tax adjustment and the legal fees.

By decision of the American justice, Elvira is forced to leave the USA.

The charge of complicity in tax fraud was not retained against her, but her presence on American territory is no longer desired.

For a person who wanted to live her American dream, the turn of events seems to put everything in question.

Bad calculation.

The sprinkler is sprinkled.

Big disappointment. Big anger against herself.

Her bitterness is indescribable.

The ex Elvira AZAROV asks and obtains the divorce.

She leaves the United States with her new identity, a brand new American passport, the remainder of the sale of the Russian bar and the VOLGA grocery store, her savings hidden from the tax authorities. This allowed her to settle in France without too much difficulty and live happily ever after.

36

Upon her arrival in France, Elvira Walker decided to settle in Grasse.

She opened a very successful painting gallery, which allowed her to build up an impressive address book in record time.

Several years passed.

By the game of remission of sentences, Andrei AZAROV is released and immediately expelled from the USA to his country of origin, Russia.

From the Ukraine, where he is originally from, Andrei sets out to find his ex-wife.

He contacts several friends in various countries, and finally locates Elvira in France, more precisely in Grasse.

At first, he went to Marseille, a city in which he created with some friends, a company of construction of individual houses.

At this same period, curiously, Elvira crosses the path of Joseph PLYNN on vacation in Grasse.

Upon his arrival in Grasse, Joseph had been taken by a bulimia of activities, which led him in turn to museums, painting galleries, Cannes, etc. ... .

During a vernissage, Elvira noticed him.

A discreet investigation allowed her to know precisely who Joseph PLYNN was. She knows all his facts and gestures. She knows everything about him.

Her desire to live the American dream is still alive in her mind.

If she cannot live it on American soil, she might as well choose an American to live it by her side, she says to herself.

Simplistic reasoning, but sincere and almost moving. She firmly believes in her dream. Nothing can stop her from turning her dream into a tangible reality.

She waits for the right moment to get in touch with the one of her dreams, this pure American on whom she bases so much hope.

One day, by the most curious of coincidences, Elvira met Andrei in a shopping mall.

Big panic.

She asks herself a thousand and one

questions.

Was it a chance meeting?
Programmed reappearance?
Since when does he observe her?
Is he armed?
Is her life in danger?
Did he come to kill her?
What is he doing in Grasse if not to find her?
Is he here to avenge the affront concerning the denunciation to the tax authorities?
Does he know the truth?

Her brain is in turmoil.

But, listening only to her courage, and to have the clear heart on his real intentions, she approaches Andrei by wearing a tense smile:

"*Oh what a nice surprise!*"

"*Hello Elvira*" he answers coldly.

"*Hello Andrei*".

"*How is business at the head of your gallery?*"

"Good! Have you been released?"

"Yes, as you can see."

"And since when?"

"For six months."

"And it's only now that you come to see me?" she said hypocritically.

"Better late than never. Isn't it?"

"Yes indeed! ... And what do you live on? Do you have a job?"

"I was kind of counting on you... You know what I mean?"

"Yes! ... I'll present you the accounts as soon as you want .... Where can I reach you?"

"We could meet at the villa. If you don't mind."

"No, not at the villa. Not at the moment. At the gallery if you want."

"When?"

"In two or three days, while I go to the safe to get the documents and some cash. OKAY?"

"Goodbye Elvira!"

With these words, Andrei AZAROV walked away without turning around.

Elvira stood there for a moment, trying to regain her composure. She was afraid. Very afraid. She is still shaking. She needs a drink. Quickly!

37

The meeting took place at the gallery as agreed.

The accounts are correct and the cash is the balance from the sale of the Russian bar and the VOLGA grocery store.

But Andrei does not (at all) seem satisfied. Something is missing.

"Do you know who turned me in?" he asks,

staring into his ex's eyes.

"***How should I know?***" answers Elvira with great confidence.

Andrei stares at her in the eyes for a long time.

Elvira supports his glance. She does not want to lower her eyes. She doesn't want to give the impression that she is involved in this story in any way.

Then she adds:

"***I had a hard time in the prosecutor's office....I can never forget those hard hours during which, I thought my life was going to go to hell....And why do you think I was expelled from the country if I had been the crow that denounced you?***"

Andrei does not answer. Then :

"***Why did you change your name?***"

Elvira does not know what to answer.

"*WALKER, isn't it?*" adds Andrei.

"*Yes!*" answers Elvira.

"*Is this before or after my incarceration in the federal prison?*" asks Andrei.

"*Before or after, what does it matter? ... I didn't know what I was doing anymore. ... I needed to get out of this mess. ... Do you think it was easy for me?*" she concludes with a half-choked voice.

"*Don't you think I have a share in your gallery and in your villa? ... It's a little thanks to my money that you could afford all this, no? ... Am I right ? So, here is what we are going to do ...* "

Very calmly, Andrei dictates his requirements.

A share in the gallery, participation in the profits of the sales with a monthly minimum, free use of the villa, invitation of his friends to stay in the villa, participation in the profits in case of rent or sale of the villa, share in the largesse of the lovers ....

It's take it or leave it.

To run the risk of seeing him destroy all that she has fought for all these years, is above her strength.

She is not willing to lose what she has taken so long to achieve, neither the painting gallery nor the villa.

Added to that, her freedom (her most precious possession) is not for sale.

So in order not to anger him further, to avoid an even more invasive intrusion in all the other compartments of her life (conditions for the acquisition of her new identity, ...) and to have peace, she compromises.

Her abnegation goes as far as accepting to sleep with him again, even if she remembers a particularly brutal man in bed, a man soaked in vodka from morning to night who doesn't care about the well-being of his wife.

He knew neither the preliminaries, nor the

caresses. A real brute.

When he managed to get an erection (usually of short duration), Elvira always had to be ready for an immediate, brutal, painful penetration.

It always ended in tears, and long minutes curled up in a hot bath trying to heal the bruised tissue.

She remembers a man who repeatedly defiled her by forcing her to have sex with two or three of his friends.

From time to time, she was forced to share her bed with real prostitutes, brought home to improve the ordinary, as he liked to say.

And it was she who was required to wash the soiled sheets and do the housework.

To his credit, he had never laid a hand on her.

Ah the perfect gentleman !!!!!

He just threatened her all day long. She couldn't say anything. The gentleman knows people, it seems. Moreover, he had her passport.

In spite of the reminiscence of all these painful memories, she accepts this new sacrifice while knowing what she exposes herself to, but refuses categorically to remarry with him.

She has other projects.

From then on, all current and future events are subject to Andrei's approval and he has the right to decide what should be and what should not be.

Thus, the project named "Joseph PLYNN" has received his approval and Elvira's plan has been reviewed and corrected.

He wants to make the most of it. He wants to rebuild his financial health thanks to the (supposedly acquired) largesse of Joseph PLYNN.

He will stop at nothing to bring this project to fruition in which he sees himself as the great organizer.

38

Robert examines the photos brought back by the private detective.

He wanted to know.

Now that he knows, what should he do with this information?

He is perplexed.

He feels both a certain shame for his father's violated honor and a real concern for the family's safety.

He imagines the worst.

He measures the extent of the disaster caused by this marriage which does not look like anything.

He has already had to deal with this famous chief of works.
He is a disreputable and potentially dangerous man.

He felt it during their face to face in his office.

Talking to Ann about it, is probably not the best solution.

Ann doesn't know how to step back and assess a situation.

Ann is a frontal person.

She is capable of flying back to confront

Elvira a second time on her home turf.

But in this kind of case, you have to keep a cool head, even if it is not a trivial situation to know that your own father is a cuckold.

Robert feels alone. He feels a certain uneasiness. He feels powerless.

Yet he has to find a solution, and quickly.

To begin with, he needs to know the exact nature of the herbal tea he has entrusted to the pharmacist.

Yes, that's where we have to start. Find out if this herbal tea is a danger to his father's health.

Robert needs irrefutable proof to confound his stepmother and force her to leave.

Therefore, he leaves his office and goes to the pharmacist.

He queues up at the end of the morning.

Finally his turn.

He asks to see the pharmacist, busy in the pharmacy.

Finally he arrives.

"Good morning, sir!"

"Good morning! What can I do for you?"

"Do you have the results of what I asked you?"

"Yes, one moment please."

The pharmacist went back into the back of the pharmacy and returned a moment later. He invites Robert to stand at the end of the counter for more discretion.

He holds an envelope in his hand, which he opens. He pulls out a paper that he unfolds. He puts on his glasses, looks at the content of the paper and then :

"Eleutherococcus senticosus. Yes, that's

right."

"What? What are you saying?" asks Robert.

"It's Siberian ginseng."

"What is it?" insists Robert.

"A stimulant of the central nervous system... An anti-hypnotic, a hypertensive among other things... It improves physical and mental performance", explains the pharmacist.

"Are you the one taking it?" The pharmacist adds

"No, it's my father," answered Robert in a dead voice.

"I hope your father doesn't have high blood pressure," warned the pharmacist.

"I don't know. What if he does?" worries Robert as he begins to understand the situation.

"*Simply put, it would drastically reduce his life expectancy. Do you understand what I mean?*" replies the pharmacist.

"*Yes, I do,*" says Robert.

39

Back home, Robert calls his father and asks him to have lunch with him.

Not this week. Elvira is coming home from a trip at the end of the week, and he has a lot of things to deal with before she gets back.

Before hanging up, he asks him :

"How are you Dad? Everything is ok?"

Joseph senses something unusual in his son's voice.

"Why this question?"

"I just want to hear from you about your health."

"Well ... For some time now, I have been feeling very tired. ... I'm breathless at the slightest effort ... I think I must consult a doctor."

« *Do it very quickly, please !* » insists Robert.

« *Don't worry, my dear son ! I'm solid as a rock* » replies Joseph in a reassuring tone.

« *A last question, Dad : do you regularly check your blood pressure ?* »

« *Not really … I don't have time to worry about that. But the last time, the results were not glorious.* » .

« *Would you like me to make an*

256   Elvira PLYNN Greatness & Decadence

appointment with the cardiologist ? »

« *Why not ? But not now. I'm very busy. …* *Robert, a question in my turn : what makes you so worried ?* »

Robert hesitates to answer, then:

« *I must confess something Dad.* »

« *Ah ? What do you mean ?* »

« *Dad, do you remember the box of Russian herbal tea ?* »

« *Yes I do.* »

« *I asked the pharmacist in my neighborhood to analyze the content.* »

« *So what?* »

« *To tell things simply, if you suffer from hypertension, you should not consume this herbal tea. Do you understand what I'm explaining to you ?* »

« *Really ?* »

« Dad, I would have liked not to have to reveal all this to you. You can believe me. »

«To tell the truth, my blood pressure is not good. … What can I do against it ? And if that's how I must go to join Barbara, I'm ready. I miss her so very much.» adds Joseph a bit fatalistic.

After a few seconds of silence, Joseph continues:

« … I think this marriage was the most serious mistake I have have made in my life …. I know how much I have deceived you and how much you have suffered … I beg your pardon … I feel so guilty for all this mess … »

Robert is overwhelmed with emotion. He has tears in his eyes.

Joseph continues:

« I made the decision to divorce. I have not announced it yet to Elvira. »

« *Good decision !* » replies Robert half relieved.

Joseph is full of words.

« *You know Robert, there are two forces that no human being on this earth can fight : habit and love.   ... I loved your mom passionately. ... No woman in the world can make me forget your mother. ... She's so present in my life. ... I feel her presence more and more around me. ... I even see her in my bedroom. ... She's peacefull. ... She seems patient. ...   She's waiting. ... She's waiting for me.* »

« *Really ?* » asks Robert.

« *Oh Yes Robert, That's true !* »   replies Joseph sure of his affirmation.

After finishing his conversation with his father who promised to call him every morning until Elvira returns, Robert doesn't feel well.

He has like a premonition.

As if history is going to repeat itself.

He doesn't know when or how it will happen.

He does not know if, at the fateful moment, he will be able to bear another blow of fate.

He has not yet digested the disappearance of his mother, even if today, he carries on his shoulders, the destiny of the PLYNN family.

40

Two days before the end of the week, Joseph has not called his son all day, as agreed.

After several unsuccessful phone attempts, Robert decides to go to the apartment.

Before leaving, he called for help.

When he arrived at the apartment, the

Elvira PLYNN Greatness & Decadence

emergency services were already there.

Robert rings several times.

There is no answer.

Then, he uses the key that his father had entrusted to him, and opens the door.

He enters the apartment first.

With a hesitant step, he moves towards the bedroom, followed by the rescue workers.

He opens the bedroom door.

His heart is beating at a thousand miles an hour.

He presses the light switch.

The room lights up.

The room is empty.

He goes out of the room and rushes to the toilet.

No one is there.

All the rooms of the apartment are inspected one after the other. In vain.

The rescuers left with Robert's apologies. They do not blame him.

Robert stayed in the apartment for a while, then decided to return to Chantilly

At the same time in Kentucky, Ann returns from an outside appointment.

When she entered his office, she got the shock of her life.

Joseph is sitting in one of the visitor's chairs with his back to the door.

Ann freezes. She doesn't understand. Yes, it is her father. Even from behind, she would recognize him between thousand.

« *Dad ?* » she said breathlessly.

« *Yes, it's me ! Hello !* »   Joseph replies

calmly, rotating his chair to face her.

« ***What are you doing here ?*** »
asks Ann very worried.

Joseph gets up and kisses his daughter, hugging her very tightly.

He smiles. He looks amused to see his daughter in all her states. But very quickly, he becomes serious again and declares:

« ***I'm putting my house in order. So, I start here. … It was here that everything began*** » replies Joseph.

That said, he resettles in the chair.

Ann puts her bag on the desk, puts her purse in the closet, and does the same.

On the other side of the desk, she faces her father.

Before anything else, she picks up her phone, asks her secretary to cancel all appointments for the day and not to disturb her under any circumstances.

They never take their eyes off each other.

Joseph seems to be filling up with the image of his daughter's face. It is as if this is the last time he will see her.

Ann tries to understand what her father has come to tell her.

Her heart is pounding.

Joseph continues to smile.

"*What do you mean, Dad?*" asks Ann.

Joseph doesn't answer. Instead, he says:

"*Could you come with me to the giant sequoia as soon as you can?...I have to go and visit an old friend.*"

Ann understands half-heartedly what her father has just said.

« *We could go as soon as you want* » replies Ann.

« *OK, thanks ! Can we go now ?* »

« *Yes, Dad ! Sure !* »

So Joseph and his daughter Ann go to Mammoth Cave National Park around the giant redwood.

Joseph leans against the giant redwood and slides down to the ground.

Ann kneels down beside him.

"*I miss you darling! ... How I miss you!*"
 says Joseph with a sob.

He remained silent for a moment, then:

"*Darling! Yes, I did a big bullshit by remarrying. But, I took the firm decision to divorce. As soon as it's done, I'll come to join you.*"

Ann can't believe her ears.

"*Really, Dad ? You want to divorce ?*" asks

Ann.

*"**The earliest would be best!**"* confirms Joseph.

*"**Oh great! I'm so happy!**"* exclaims Ann.

Then, patiently, methodically, Joseph tells of Robert's discovery. He also expresses his concern about his failing health. He feels unhealthy. He doesn't know if he will survive all these events. That is why it is important for him to get his affairs in order.

Ann listens to her father without interrupting him.
After he has finished telling her what he has been through since his remarriage to Elvira, Joseph adds this terse, but pregnant sentence:

« *Ann, we'll meet again soon in France* »

41

After this moment of intense emotions in the park, Ann accompanies her father to her house to take a little rest.

Joseph must return to France in two days.
It is thus prudent to take some strength before crossing again the ocean to France.

But before going to bed, he asks Ann to

Elvira PLYNN Greatness & Decadence

inform Robert of his little escapade in America.

Ann tells her brother what she has just experienced.

Robert could not believe it, but was relieved to know that he was with his sister.

Both of them think that the most reasonable thing to do is to prevent him from returning to France.

But both of them know perfectly well their father's determination.

Joseph is not the kind of person to shy away.

He wants to announce his decision to his future ex-wife himself. He does not want to hide behind a lawyer to accomplish what he believes to be his duty.

Knowing his father's intentions, Robert believes he is now authorized to build a case to force his stepmother to accept the divorce without making a scandal or demanding a moral reparation that would be prohibitive.

He feels revived.

The decision of his father to separate from this woman who is the devil incarnate, allows him to foresee the future of the family unit under better omens.

He is filled of joy to know that his father did not forget his mother. He talked about it with Ann. It gave them a lot of hope.

He has only one thing in mind now, to go and pick up his father at the airport to give him a full report on his research, and to discuss together how to implement the decision.

The day Joseph returned to France, Robert went to the airport to meet his father.

He waits patiently.

The plane is announced.

The plane lands at the scheduled time.
The passengers disembark.

The passengers leave one by one.

No Joseph in sight.

The last passenger of the flight has just left.

Robert waits a few more minutes.

He calls Ann.

Ann confirms that Joseph has taken the plane to Paris.

Big concern in Kentucky.

Robert loses his footing.

He goes to the counter of the American company that has chartered the flight from the United States.

He introduced himself and explained his problem.

The lady at the counter asks him for an ID. Then, she picks up the phone, talks for a while with the person on the other end of the line, and hangs up.

She invites him to wait a moment.

A few moments later, a man and a woman arrive at the counter, greet him and ask him to follow them.

They take him into an office, seat him and then tell him the sad news.

At the time of disembarkation, the flight crew noted the death of Mr. Joseph PLYNN, a first class passenger on the Louisville - Paris flight from Louisville International Airport.

According to the initial findings of the airport doctor, Joseph PLYNN suffered a heart attack while sleeping. He did not suffer.

At the request of the public prosecutor, the body is transferred to the forensic institute of Paris, to be autopsied.

Robert is devastated. He does not know what to say. He is overwhelmed. He stays in the company office for a while, then, after receiving the last instructions to approach the French and American authorities, Robert finally leaves the office and heads for a bar inside the airport.

He orders a double whiskey.

He can't drink it.

The last time he drank a whiskey was with his father in Grasse.

42

« ***Hello , Ann ?*** »

« ***Yes Robert, You found him ?*** »　Ann worries.

« ***Yes I did !*** »　replies Robert who struggles to tell her the bad news.

« ***Good, where was he ?*** »　asks Ann, eager to know.

« *Ann, …. »*

Robert can't tell her.

« *Robert, please, what happens ? … please, telle me ! Please …. »* insists Ann.

« *Dad is dead. I am so sorry. »* says Robert who bursts into tears.

Ann bursts into tears in turn.

After a while :

« *Does Shirley know what happened ? »* Ann asks between two sobs.

« *Not yet. I don't know how to tell her »* confesses Robert.

« *Don't worry Robert, I'll call her. You, you're in charge of calling Elvira. Yes ? »*

He hangs up. He takes the glass of whiskey and makes a toast:

« *Cheers ! »*

Then he drinks the glass in one go.

Robert returns to Chantilly.

Shirley and her girlfriend come to greet him in the courtyard.

They fall into each other's arms.

They cry, and cannot stop crying.

The atmosphere is heavy with sadness.

An era is coming to an end.

History has repeated itself.

They are now in a hand-to-hand struggle with their destiny.

They end up calming down. A moment later, they go back inside and gather in their father's room.

This room in which, he had taken refuge because he could not support any more to see the belongings of Barbara which brought back too many memories to him.

Shirley clutches her brother's arm. She's afraid he'll leave too.

Ann did her best to reassure her, but in vain.

She is traumatized.

Robert tries to reassure her as best he can. But, two successive blows of the fate, finished by having reason of her confidence in the future.

She is in an indescribable panic.

She is afraid of sinking into madness.

She wants to return to the United States, to her sister.
Nobody wants to have dinner.

But before going to bed, Robert sends a telephone message to Elvira in Grasse to tell her that her father has died.

The message will reach her the next morning.

In Paris, the day after the death of Joseph PLYNN, a hard day is coming.

Robert must go to the forensic institute to formally recognize the body of his father.

Shirley offers to accompany him.

At the same time in Grasse, Elvira receives a message by phone.

She listens to it until the end without flinching.

She turns to Andrei and says:

"*That's it!*"

She doesn't need to say anything more.

Andrei goes to the kitchen and brings back a bottle of champagne.

He opens it and fills two glasses.

He makes a toast. They toast. They drink.

"*You see, it pays to have let the body of this old man lie on you and penetrate you with his old penis. ... You didn't want to. ... You saw, it didn't last long. ... As soon as you return, make the box of herbal tea disappear. It is essential! Do you understand? If not, you know what awaits you...* " adds Andrei.

Elvira listens to him without replying.

She is worried about her return to Paris. She must participate in the organization of the funeral and assert her rights to the inheritance.

43

Back home after this day marked by the burial of her husband, Elvira, a recent widow, settled down for a few moments in one of the armchairs of the living room, still dressed in black, a glass of cognac in her hand.

She is trying to decompress after this "supposed" ordeal.

She is waiting for a phone call from Andrei.

He must come to join her at the apartment after the funeral.

She doesn't want to stay there alone.

A few minutes later, as she tries to clear her mind, and evaluate the other steps to come to complete what she has started, she suddenly remembers, that the box of herbal tea bags was not thrown away as her ex-husband Andrei recommended.

She rushes to the kitchen.

She opens the cupboard.

She frantically looks for the box of herbal tea.

It is not any more in its place.

She does not understand.

Big panic.
She searches again and again.

She searches in all the cupboards. Maybe it has been moved. One never knows.

Nothing!

She returns to sit in the armchair.

The doorbell rings.

Finally Andrei! she says to herself. She is relieved.

She gets up and goes to open the door.

She opens the door.

No one!

She examines the corridor from left to right: nobody.

An icy air current coming from nowhere, envelops her from head to foot.

She has goose bumps. She shivers. She closes the door hastily and returns to sit down in the living room, trying to remember where she could have stored the box of herbal tea bags.

The apartment is empty. There is nobody there but her.

Yet she has the unpleasant impression that she is not alone. She feels a presence at her side.

She desperately waits for Andrei's arrival.

But, Andrei does not come.

She wonders.

Then, drunk of alcohol and tiredness, Elvira ends up falling asleep in the armchair.

In the early morning, she is awakened by an urge to relieve herself.

After that, she regains the marital room.

She remembers again the flaccid body of the old man near whom, she spent so many nights by tightening the fists.

She remembers his hot breath in her neck as he tried to penetrate her but failed.

She remembers how many times she had to change the sheets because the old man failed to penetrate her.

She remembers his breath reeking of whiskey.

How many moments of life sacrificed on behalf of her dream!

If she had to do it again, she doesn't want to go through the same thing again. She feels no nostalgia.

In her head, an obsession: how to recover the apartment, put it on sale and leave the country?

Will she have to hire a lawyer, or negotiate with Robert?

She has not forgotten his conciliatory attitude, taking up the cause for her in

Grasse, whereas Ann did not want to hear about her.

But is Robert still her ally?

The episode of the chief of works coming to claim money from Joseph, perhaps, altered his opinion and his benevolence towards her.

She needs to know if Robert is still the person she could manipulate to her liking at that time before her marriage, to serve her interests.

She no longer wants to live in France.

For her, France is over!

She decides to take a bath.

She removes her makeup while the bathtub fills with water and scented foam.

As soon as she gets in the tub, she hears the doorbell ring.

She hesitates.

It could be Andrei.

So she quickly puts on a robe and rushes to the door.

She opens the door.

In front of her, two policemen came to give her a summons in person.

They take leave.

Elvira closes the door.

She frantically opens the envelope, then takes note of the wording of the convocation.

The reason of the convocation :

"*Matter concerning you*".

She becomes nervous. Extremely nervous.

Should she go to this summons?

Will she go to this convocation?

She picks up the phone and calls Andrei at his hotel in Saint-Lazare.

The receptionist tells her that Mr. AZAROV has left the hotel since the end of yesterday without leaving any address.

She puts the phone down and picks it up again.

She dials the number of the villa in Grasse and leaves several messages just in case.

Indeed, Andrei returned to the villa.

He ends up calling her back.

She doesn't have time to make a scene for not having kept his promise to spend the night with her at the apartment.

She is satisfied to explain him the urgency and the gravity of the situation.

She waits for his instructions before going to the convocation at 2 p.m .

Against any waiting, and before anything, Andrei takes news of the box of sachets of herbal tea.

She admits to him the disappearance of the box. She does not know where it went.

Andrei just promises to call her back later.

Elvira hangs up the telephone, half reassured.

Andrei hurriedly tidied up his belongings, closed the villa, got into his car and drove to Marseille, leaving behind him an indescribable mess.

The nightmare continues.

She remembers the long hours spent at the financial division of the prosecutor's office in New York, answering the same questions over and over again.

All this past (not so distant), comes back in her memory as if by magic.

She doesn't want this anymore.

She goes back to the bathroom to finish her toilet, in a total discomfort, without really knowing what she is doing.

Her face accuses the blow.

In front of the mirror, she tries to arrange her face with a bit of makeup and some strokes of pencil here and there. She tries to restore her former splendor evaporated in one night.

She dresses soberly and goes to install herself near the telephone.

10:30 a.m .

No call.

Midday.

No call.

She begins to despair.

She feels hypoglycemic.

She needs to eat something.

She prepares herself a plate of salmon and some blinis, an old food habit acquired in the days of the Volga grocery store.

She pours herself a big glass of Chardonnay.

She continues to wait.

Still no call.

1:30 p.m .

She sets out with a hesitant step.

She arrives at the police station.

She shows her summons.
The agent at the reception desk informs the commander.

A few moments later, the commander comes to take her to his office.

While getting inside the room, Elvira sees on

the desk of the commander, the box of sachets of herbal tea.

PART 2

(The end of the American Dream)

« The culprit goes to his punishment like water to the sea, like the offended to his revenge... » (Amélie NOTHOMB)

Elvira PLYNN Greatness & Decadence

Elvira PLYNN Greatness & Decadence

44

In the commander's office, Elvira is asked to sit down.

The commander goes around the table, opens a cupboard, takes out a file contained in a red folder and puts it on the desk.

From her chair, Elvira manages to read:

 "Joseph PLYNN / Handrail."

Her blood freezes.

Before anything else, the commander offers her a cup of coffee.

Elvira declines the offer, secretly preferring a glass of vodka, and incidentally knowing not the object of the convocation, but what the red file contains.

"*Sincere condolences.*" whispers the commander while finishing to settle at his desk.

"*Thank you! ... It's nice of you,*" replies Elvira politely.

"*It's normal,*" replies the commander.

She doesn't care about his condolences. She is eager to know why she is in this place.

"*Excuse me!*" says the commander before getting up and leaving the office.

Elvira can't stand it anymore.

She cannot resist the urge to get up, walk around the desk and open the file.

But, as soon as thought, as soon forgotten because, the commander regains his office before she had time to carry out her plan.

Missed!

The commander settles in his chair, finishes his coffee and then :

*"**Madam, do you know why you are here?**"*

*"**No! ... I just buried my husband as you know. And I don't know what I'm doing here**"* answers Elvira with a false assurance that betrays her shaky voice.

*"**Don't you have a little idea?**"* insists the commander.

*"**No!**"* answers Elvira with a closed face.

The commander grabs the red file and opens it. He flips through the ten or so pages that the file contains. He takes his time. He takes all his time. Then:

*"**Before dying your late husband came to***

the police station to deposit a handrail" specifies the commander who continues to read jumbled the sheets of the file.

Elvira does not answer.

"*Does it speak to you?*" insists the commander.

"*No, I don't see why he would have come to file a report. You know he's a businessman ... Maybe it's an action related to his business. Who knows? ... I don't know what to tell you. Really, I don't know what I'm doing here. ... I'm unable to answer you. ... Then tell me what you know.*"

The perfidious Elvira!

The commander is red with anger and changes his tone.

"*It is me who asks the questions, and it is up to you to bring me answers. You understood me well?*" he adds dryly.

No answer.

Elvira wallows in silence.

"*You understood me well?*" insists the commander.

"*Yes! yes!*" finally answers Elvira, quite annoyed.

"*Good! Let's start again: do you know why Mr. Joseph PLYNN came to deposit a handrail?*"

"*No! How should I know? He didn't tell me anything. He doesn't talk to me about his business*", answers Elvira.

The commander takes the red file. He pulls out a sheet, then:

"*Tell me about yourself.*"

"*What do you want to know?*" asks Elvira.

"*For example, your identity. The real one.*" answers the commander.

After a moment of hesitation:

"*Elvira PLYNN, formerly Elvira WALKER.*"

"*And Elvira AZAROV, it was in another life? What happened in the United States? How did you go from AZAROV to WALKER?*" adds the commander impatient to hear her explanation.

Elvira does not know what to answer.

"*Could I have a glass of water, please?*" implores Elvira.

The commander gets up, walks out of the office and returns with half a bottle of spring water purchased from the vending machine.

"*Would you like a glass?*"

"*No, it's fine, thanks.*"

Elvira absorbs the contents of the half-bottle in one go.

She catches her breath.

She wipes her lips with the paper handkerchief she has been fiddling with since she arrived at the police station.

She is stunned.

The nightmare continues.

"*So?*" insists the commander who raises his voice.

45

Sitting facing the commander, Elvira cannot hide her discomfort.

Her legs are driven by sudden and irregular movements.

Her knees knock together.

Her whole body, traversed of jolts, expresses her uneasiness in front of this situation in which she plays big.

She would like to be elsewhere. But she cannot.

Her mind can hide behind convolutions, but her body cannot escape.

The cards that chance has just dealt her, do not include any major figure giving her the possibility to overturn the table.

The world collapses around her.

She tries to regain her composure.

She has to refocus mentally, in order to be able to formulate the answers expected by the commander. Credible answers, as possible as she can.

It is imperatively necessary, insofar as, the questioning of the commander puts back in light all the troubled past which she tries desperately to hide since so many years.

For her, there is no useful universal truth.

Her truth is the one that must be dressed in light to enlighten the most suspicious of men.

So, pretending not to forget any detail, Elvira tries everything.

She tells a cock-and-bull story, a narrative in which, sequences of life which took place in the United States follow one another, in particular her brief marriage with a certain Jeremy Walker prematurely recalled to God following a cancer of the testicles, etc...

The commander listens without flinching.

He is limited to transcribe the allegations of this woman ready to do anything to get out of it.

In twenty years of career, he have seen all kinds of diversionary attempts.

For the moment, he is content to take her statement, knowing that information from the New York prosecutor's office will come in the next few hours to corroborate or refute the allegations of the former Mrs. AZAROV.

The commander interrupts the transcription of the deposition several times.

Indeed, the exceptionally high level of imagination and the capacity of improvisation of Elvira do not cease to amaze this experienced confrontation specialist.

If only he could be convinced.

The box of tissues is not far away.

Elvira is at the top of her art.

She has to save her head. She knows it.

But soon the commander resumes the routine of transcribing the statement and continues the hearing with more and more targeted questions.

Suddenly, Elvira collapses on her chair.

For a few seconds, the commander believes in a simulation, but, in front of the spectacle of her convulsing body, he picks up his telephone and calls the help.

When the emergency services arrived, the visual elements observed (eyes revolting, drooling, stiff body, ...) allowed the following diagnosis: epileptic seizure.

Elvira suffers of this pathology since her childhood. Her seizures were frequent, as soon as she was subjected to a strong emotion.

But in adolescence, the seizures became less frequent.

She has learned to hide what she considers to be a defect by controlling her emotions in all circumstances, no matter where they come from.

To keep it from coming out, Elvira would break off relationships with her schoolmates who knew her secret.

As soon as she could, she left her native Normandy for the south of France before migrating to the United States.

Thus, she thought, her secret was well kept by bridging the gap between her former life and the one that lay ahead in the United States.

To stay or to go, to change or to get used to, Elvira's choices have always been conditioned by the permanent concern of erasing to the last line, the imperfections that denature her physical body, likely to influence the realization of her dreams, as well as the opportunities that mark her road through life.

Until today, the long succession of choices in her life, is a mixture of disasters, absurdities, inconsistencies.

The reasons?

Elvira is a concentrate of paradoxes in her way of apprehending life.
Sometimes her critical mind is at its most relevant, thus avoiding the worst pitfalls, other times (most often), her reasoning, altered

by her certainties and greed, leads her inexorably towards the densest darkness, from where she has difficulty in seeing the light at the end of the tunnel.

46

The Parisian hospital where Elvira is admitted after her epileptic seizure in the commander's office is not subject to any specific security measures.

Elvira is in a unit under the neurology department, located a little away from the other departments.
In this unit, Elvira is considered no more and

no less than an ordinary patient in crisis, admitted to receive appropriate care.

As such, she is not subject to any restriction of personal freedom.

There are no police officers in front of her room.

No charge is retained against her. At least, for the moment.

Elvira comes back to herself little by little.

She observes the white ceiling, the neon lamp, the grey walls, the bars in front of the big glass windows, ...

Nobody around her. Just a table and a chair.

At first, she tries to understand the reasons of her presence in this place.

Little by little, her mind becomes clearer.

She remembers this merciless commander with whom she was in conversation in his office.

Correction: she was answering the commander's questions.

She does not remember anything else.

The reason of her presence in this place, escapes her completely.

For the moment she remains prostrate in her bed.

She tries to put back together the fragments of memories which populate her mind.

Yes! she remembers now the reason of her presence in this place.

What she has always considered as a defect, has just saved her life.

Her epileptic seizure has just freed her from the sharp claws of the police commander.

What an irony of fate!

We don't always want what happens to us, but how can we not feel completely indebted to this irony of fate, which is undeniably the hidden face of our destiny, or at least one of its components?

Taken by a sudden urge, she manages to get down from this high hospital bed.

She opens one of the two doors at the back of the room.

Wrong! This door is the one of the cupboard.

She opens the second one, located just next to it.

Good catch.

After having relieved this sudden urge, Elvira returns in the room.

She goes towards the door of the cupboard. She opens it. She stops. She thinks.

Machinally, she takes again her clothes and dresses without hurrying.

She puts on her shoes. She is ready.

She seizes her bag, checks summarily the contents. Everything is there: the keys, ... , and the most important, her American passport.

One last look at her hair. No time to look for the comb at the bottom of the bag and to fix it. Her fingers do the trick.

Like a visitor, Elvira leaves her room. She goes towards the elevators. She waits in the stream of visitors.

This is the last image of Elvira captured by the service's cameras.

47

The absence of the patient of the room 19 was not observed.

Indeed, the arrival of the night team creates the ideal conditions of floating within the service, supporting the disappearance of Elvira without any alarm being triggered.

A quick trip to the apartment, then, direction the Lyon train station where she takes a train to the south of France.

There is no question of taking a plane. It is necessary to avoid to let traces. She must muddy the waters.

Facing herself in this train that speeds through the French countryside, and which (she hopes) will lead her to her freedom, like a condemned woman, she sees her life flash before her eyes.

This accelerated film of the events that have marked her life, which make her a true criminal in every sense of the word, before God and before men, gives her a glimpse for the first time of the kind of woman she has become.

What a pedigree!

She does not want to die fighting.

She prefers to stay alive by running away.

For the moment, this attitude fits perfectly with her idea of her immediate future: to stay free no matter what.

Brave, but not reckless.

She doesn't have the time to look in that rearview mirror to see her entire past.

She cannot afford the luxury of introspection and accept the verdict.

As for remorse, we'll see later, especially since this word is not part of her vocabulary.

She is neither amnesic of this past (not so distant), nor inclined to search at all costs for the reasons of this slippage in her life course.

Who is to blame?   (A million dollar question indeed!)

To this mother who one day revealed to her daughter who her real father was?
Or, to this American student who got a young French woman pregnant, and who left at the end of his studies without looking back?

315   Elvira PLYNN Greatness & Decadence

Can all this explain her devouring passion for the Americas?

What is behind this feverish quest that has been driving her since her adolescence, since her mother's confession?

Is it the desire that has been hidden in her for all these years, a desire that she assimilates to her will to collect the repayment of a supposed moral debt contracted towards her by this American student a few months before her birth, a moral debt that became due the day she was born?

Futile reasoning? Preposterous attitude?

What does it matter!

The whole tragedy of her life is based on this certainty which, over time, has become for her a universal truth.

Through her perception of the elements linked to the particular conditions of her birth, her mind reassures her as much as she can, and finds a just reason for this gap between good and evil that never ceases to widen.

Here she is now in the clothes of a fugitive who (it is true), has a length before her pursuers. Her steel horse is out of reach for the moment.

48

From Cannes to Grasse, Elvira makes the trip by cab.

While waiting for the opening of the banks to go to her safe, she prepares two suitcases which she leaves in the vestibule.

She allows herself a few hours of rest,

sleeping on one ear, watching for the slightest noise.

The cracks of the wood of the frame in the silence of the night, until then without effect on her, are now, a source of concern since her return to the villa.

She is startled by the slightest noise.

However, it is necessary that she sleeps. She has to recover from her epileptic seizure.

The day that is about to dawn is likely to be very trying.

The villa is still in an indescribable mess.

Andrei having paid nothing to the workmen of the hundred thousand euros extorted from the late Joseph. PLYNN, because of this the building site is at a complete stop.

According to the last news, he is in Marseille.

In the early morning, Elvira woke up in pain. Her mock night was not enough to bring her the restful rest she needed.

An express shower, a frugal breakfast, here she is on the war foot, waiting for the opening of her bank to recover cash and her jewels.

She remains locked up inside. There is no question of her being seen in the garden.

There is no need to quarrel with luck.

So far, it seems to be on her side.

For more discretion, the shutters of the villa remain closed.

She does not know how to occupy herself while waiting for the opening of the banks. She is like a lioness in a cage.

She turns on the television. Nothing interesting. Cartoons.

She flips from channel to channel.
She finally turns off the set.

She looks at her watch.

7:30 a.m ! The time is definitely slow.

8:30 a.m . Finally!

In a quarter of an hour, she will leave the villa with her luggage.

She will take a cab that will stop at the bank.

Then, direction Ventimiglia.

Ventimiglia train station.

She pays the cab driver, who is a friend, handsomely.

A one-night stand, but a friend for life.

She knows she can count on his complete discretion.

When she unloaded her suitcases from the trunk of the cab at the Ventimiglia train station, he could not help but question her with his eyes.

He is worried.

She sketches a smile and passes her hand on his cheek.

Everything is fine, she seems to tell him.

Yet he tries to understand what is going on. He wants to understand.

He is convinced that something serious is going on. But what is it?

He knows Elvira well enough to know that sometimes, she has nothing to envy to an oyster.

She kisses him on the mouth and says before leaving him:

"*Take a look at the villa from time to time, please!*"

"*Where can I reach you just in case?*"

"*I have your number. See you soon. ...*"

*"**Be careful.**"*

*"**Don't be afraid.**"*

Elvira enters the train station.

She boards the first train to San Remo.

Elvira PLYNN Greatness & Decadence

49

San Remo train station. Last stop.

During the journey, Elvira had time to doze off for a while, her handbag (which contains a real fortune), wedged between her thigh and the window.

When she woke up, nothing to report. The

bag and its contents have not moved.

In the flow of passengers disembarking from the Ventimiglia - San Remo train, Elvira behaved like an ordinary passenger.

Very calmly, she pushes the cart on which her two suitcases are stored.

She avoids drawing attention to herself.

At the exit of the train station, she queues in front of the cab rank.

She waits patiently for her turn.

She ends up getting into a cab that takes her to the city center in search of a guesthouse.

She is lucky. The cab driver knows a boarding house, directed by a rich widow, but a bit far from the city, if the distance from the city center is not a problem for her.

It's a good thing: Elvira needs to get away from it all.

No check-in at the reception of the boarding house.

This eliminates any trace of her presence in this place.

A boarding house is the ideal place for people like her, eager to take a break and to blend in the landscape.

The boarding house, which is located in an affluent two-story building, suits her perfectly.

It is a XIX century building, inspired by the Italian renaissance architecture, in ochre color.

The widow Andreoti, who speaks half a dozen languages, is content to say hello to her and to collect the week's rent.

She gives her the rules of the residence, as well as a description of the services offered to the residents.

The only rule on which the widow Andreoti

particularly insists is the punctuality at meal times.

This takes place in the large dining room on the ground floor, at the central table around which all residents of all conditions are invited.

Another constraint: visits are forbidden inside the building, but tolerated in the park.
In addition, the stay gives the right to walk in the two-hectare park that surrounds the building, in the shade of the weeping willows that border the pond.

She feels safe in this place where no one knows her, a place where she did not have to show any identification to register.

Perfect anonymity in a perfect hideout.

Elvira can't think of anything better.

Luck continues to be on her side. But until when?
The only drawback, no bellman to take her luggage up to the second floor without an

elevator. No gentleman around to help her either.

She can't have it all. She's not in a palace.

After cashing in the week's pension and giving a commission to the cab driver, who immediately took his leave, the widow Andreoti (nicknamed Madame la Baronne) resumed reading the day's newspaper, comfortably installed in her armchair by the window.

Elvira managed to get her two suitcases into her room on the second floor.

The contents of these two suitcases represent for her, what she has of more precious, not necessarily in financial value, but in sentimental value. From the smallest panties to the most chic dress, she did not choose them at random.

She is exhausted.

She settles for a moment at the foot of the bed.

She measures the way traversed.

Her nerves give out.

She cries in silence.

She tries to calm herself. She does not succeed.

In the end, she regains her senses, determined to move forward, to take advantage of these eight days of respite in this boarding house to recover and make other plans.

Her nerves were put to the test. For her, it is a real miracle if she can now freely decide on her actions in this boarding house.

She installs her things in the old wardrobe whose door does not close properly.
Inside which smells the mildew, she puts the minimum of clothes for the week, while leaving the door open to air the interior, thus avoiding that her clothes impregnate themselves with this smell that she dislikes. To make sure her clothes don't smell like

mildew on her and make her look like an unwashed woman, she takes a portable perfume spray out of her purse and perfumes her hanging clothes.

Her panties remained in the suitcases. There is no question of storing them in this wardrobe that gives off a stench.

A soothing shower followed by a nap while waiting for dinner time.

50

Around the big table in the central room of the residence, people who seem to be "ordinary" and who, like Elvira, have probably come to this place to shelter heavy secrets.

Four women, two men and as many personal stories that each of these people carry from ancient times, and which led them to this place where the only obligation is to pay the rent at the beginning of each week.

They are people of a certain standing, almost faceless, without precise age, with nonchalant looks, translating the weight of their past which prevents them from moving with ease, in an alert way.

In the manner of a pack when a new member arrives, each one approaches to smell this new candidate for integration.

But, unlike the wolves whose alpha male, at the head of its pack, observes with attention the positioning of the ears and tail of the newcomer as a sign of submission before deciding on its fate, there is no alpha male around this table. On the other hand, Elvira doesn't know which signs, nor which pheromones she should send to this already formed group, to make herself accepted, except for the offspring of her expensive perfume. In spite of her bad character and her state of mind of the moment, her desire to melt in the mass, orders her to keep a low profile within this community which she would like to integrate for a time, for her survival in freedom. Indeed, she does not know who is who. So beware!

Seen from the outside, her face, tired by stress, does not hide the attitude of a person in distress, looking for a lost corner to hide.

In the absence of a formal introduction, then, in a conventional way, everyone at least nods to her in greeting.

She does not speak Italian. She answers them in English, (the universal language par excellence, they say), while wearing a tense smile on her lips.

But who is telling her that these residents are Italian?

Let's go around the table.

Among the four women, only one is Italian.

She came from an Italian island in the Mediterranee sea, namely Sicily. She has been living in the boarding house for about two years, following a scandal that almost cost her her life. She had cheated on her husband who had not hesitated to have her lover killed. So, she had run away, watching every day for two years, the arrival of the hitman who will finish the job. For her, every day is a day won. Every day, she adorns herself with all her jewels in case it is her last day on earth. Thus (she thought) she would leave this world, beautiful and adorned with all her jewels, some of which were given to her by her deceased lover, jewels that she particularly cherished.

The second woman was a wealthy German woman who in her heyday, was a frequent visitor to the Italian Riviera. Part of her fortune had been swallowed up in casinos. Almost ruined, and suffering from a deep chronic depression, she no longer felt able to return to Germany. So her dear old friend, « Madame la Baronne » (whom she had met in a casino in Rimini), charitably offered her free accommodation in her boarding house.

The third woman, a Spanish woman who in her youth had served in the Royal Palace of Pardo during the time of the Caudillo. After his death in 1975, she left Madrid and went into exile in Italy to finish her life. First in Rome, she lived with an Italian man (a businessman) she had met in Spain, who died a few months after their meeting, leaving her a small fortune. This was followed by a wandering through Italy that led her to San Remo. Having lived since her birth in Madrid (a landlocked city), she had chosen to live in the open air in San Remo because of its maritime location. In summer as in winter, she never left her « abanico », a precious fan adorned with fine lace, which she had received from the hands of Maria del Carmen Polo, the wife of the Caudillo.

The fourth woman, of Russian origin, is the most mysterious of all the residents. She doesn't talk to anyone, she spends her days reading in the park. No one knows where she comes from. It is whispered among the staff in charge of room maintenance that in her room there is a photo of a young teenage girl on her bedside table. No one knows what her story is. No one knows why she is not communicating. No phone calls in the last year. Never a visitor to see her in the park.

The only highlight of the week: every Friday morning she leaves the residence in a cab and returns on Saturday in the early afternoon. The speculations go on, even imagining a lover hiding in town. But nobody dares to ask her.

As for the two men, neither one has the characteristics of an alpha male.

The first is Austrian, a painter by profession, a former resident of the Villa Medici in Roma. Promised to a brilliant career, this Austrian, following a disappointment in love, lost himself in the fumes of alcohol, to the point of not being able to feel the slightest inspiration. His paintings were exhibited in major art galleries throughout Italy. He was famous and adored in the art world. Now he is only a shadow of his former self, locked in a past that meant so much to him and from which he cannot escape. From time to time, they can see him in the park, in front of his easel. His canvas remains every other day, immaculate at the end of the day because of his lack of inspiration. When he saw Elvira, he had a shock. He saw in her the perfect face that could inspire him, the kind of face he had been waiting for a long time, the trigger to resurrect his desire to paint and thus rise from his ashes. But he decided to procrastinate. He needs to take his time to study (from a distance) this face that expresses both fear and horror. Will Elvira accept to pose for him, (she who does not want to leave any trace behind her)? To be continued.

The other gentleman, an American, a former surgeon who, after a surgery that led to the death of his patient, left the United States to settle in Italy. The deceased patient was the only son of his best friend, with whom he had studied at the university. Two inseparable friends that, the death of this 14 year old teenager who underwent emergency surgery for a banal appendectomy, had separated them forever. Inconsolable since then, he had considered several times to kill himself, but each time, he lacked courage, such as that day when he did not have the courage to announce himself to his best friend, the death of his son, preferring to let the protocol of the clinic take its course in terms of communication with families in such circumstances.

51

It is 7:30 pm.

Elvira waits for everyone to settle down before taking her turn, for fear of causing trouble by occupying someone else's supposed place: habits are quickly acquired.

Emotions whet appetite, says the old adage.

She doesn't hesitate to eat her well-stocked

plate.

The opportunity to taste real Italian cuisine, compared to those dishes offered in pizzerias outside Italy.

This evening, a unique dish as at home: a large plate of spaghetti alle Vongole (pasta with clams) as a wink to the not so distant past evoking this famous dinner during which scallop nuts (which triggered this devouring passion in an American passing through Grasse), have been served, accompanied by a bottle of champagne and not a pitcher of Chianti, as it is the case at this table around which, reigns a heavy silence punctuated by the noise of cutlery touching the plates.

Nobody seems to be interested in her. She tries discreetly to scrutinize the faces of the ones and the others. Nothing can be seen through these faces captivated by the content of the plates.

Is this a good sign, in which case, she would indeed have found the right hideout.

Besides, why should there be anything to worry about? In her defense, as Jean De La Fontaine wrote:

"Mistrust is the mother of safety."

But what about this excess of prudence that would end up arousing suspicion?

Is it really in her interest to persist in this attitude that would end up being fatal for her, even if most of the boarders are not in the odor of sanctity?

For the moment, the dinner is going well. All the indicators to show her safety and well-being in this community seem to be green. As long as no one questions her about her past and the reasons for her arrival in this boarding house, instead of a chic hotel by the sea, then she should calm down and enjoy this moment of happiness shared around this well-stocked table.

She doesn't dare ask for another pitcher of Chianti. She needs to get drunk. She needs a strong alcohol. She hopes for a digestif at the end of the dinner. But no one seems to be in that same need, settling for that pitcher of Chianti classico included in the menu. Considering the situation, it is necessary to keep reason and avoid attracting the attention of her table neighbors. For tonight it will be fine, she says to herself. The next day, she will be able to buy one or two bottles of Cognac, carefully hidden in her room, if she deigns to put her nose outside, or ask (for a fee) a maid to make this purchase for her in all discretion. She has all night to think about it.

52

First night in this boarding house.

Before going to bed, a short inspection: no spiders on the ceiling, no cobwebs in the corners of the room, no suspicious stains on the sheets, but still this persistent smell of mildew escaped from the bowels of the old wardrobe despite the spraying of her favorite perfume on her clothes in the afternoon. She has a delicate sense of smell, poor girl!
The occasion for her to test in real, the

quality of the mattress. Not very good. Elvira misses her cozy bed, her silk sheets at the villa, her evening bath with its perfumed foam, her beauty products, to maintain and nourish the skin of her face, her firming creams for her body that she would always like to be slender and tonic, her glass of fresh Chardonnay on her bedside table for a sweet and light drunkenness to help her fall asleep, her remote control to frantically flick from one channel to another, comfortably installed in her bed waiting for the Chardonnay to do its effect and for Morpheus to take her in his arms.

All in all, this is perhaps better for her than the spartan and unhealthy comfort of a prison cell: promiscuity, non-existent intimacy, shower at the end of the corridor once a week, walks under regulated surveillance, psychological pressure, permanent tension between inmates, quality of the food questionable, she who likes refined, delicious and balanced food

What more can she ask for in the current conditions?

She, the fugitive who is probably the object of a search by the police in France or by

Interpol at the international level?

During this dotted night alternating long moments of wakefulness and fleeting moments of dozing, (a state close to sleep which did not allow her to regenerate and regain strength after her crazy week), Elvira (with the little energy she had left) examined her situation.

She lowers her chances of getting out of it, almost regretting her escape, when no charge was hanging over her, even if her deceased husband had registered a handrail at the police station. A handrail does not make it possible to initiate proceedings against the author of an act, but simply to inform the police of the nature and date of an act. In this case, the fact of having found a packet of Siberian Ginseng in the kitchen cupboard, could not constitute the beginning of proof that could enlighten the investigation concerning the heart attack of Joseph who suffered from hypertention and who did not have an irreproachable hygiene of life.

Elvira does not want to take more than her share in the responsibility in Joseph's death, just like Joseph's business which took all his time, and which forced him to live without worrying about his health.

Elvira finds herself in this room in Italy because in the eyes of her fellow men, she would have sinned by serving Joseph, day after day, a cup of herbal tea to boost his boldness in bed.

So this room in which she finds herself at this very moment, is it hell or purgatory?

Or is it not a place of redemption that should allow her to redeem her soul perverted by her greed?

Greedy but nevertheless fervent Christian, she thinks of the punishment of God, this subtle entity which (according to her) knows all and sees all.

For her defense, how could she know that Joseph suffered from hypertension and that ginseng was contraindicated for him as well as the little blue pill?

She regrets having carried out Andrei's orders, whose main objective was to weaken Joseph's heart so that Elvira could inherit as quickly as possible.

She also regrets her choice to take refuge in

Italy, a country that has probably signed an extradition agreement with France.

But by the way, she is not French. She is an American citizen. However, she cannot use her precious status as an American citizen.

The former Mrs. Walker, can not decently go to the U.S. Embassy in Italy to seek refuge in case of immediate need. Everyone knows why.

She had miraculously escaped from the clutches of the New York prosecutor, and she has no desire to go back there thanks to a new case relayed by the U.S. Embassy in Italy. The repatriation to the USA by special flight would be immediate. The PLYNN lawyers would be delighted.

53

At the boarding house, the days pass, the weeks follow one another, Elvira settles into a kind of routine.

Every morning, in search of the slightest information concerning her, she buys the main French newspapers.

The reading of these newspapers occupies her mornings. She can thus reassure herself and plan to spend the rest of the day in a serene way. At least, she tries to.

The highlight of the week: the Austrian painter manages to get her attention.

How did he manage to open this hermetically sealed oyster?

Simply by catching her reading an art magazine in the park.

He struck up a conversation with her and soon they realized that they shared te same passion for painting.

She knew that he was the painter Eliaz and she was honored to meet him in this very special place where everyone comes to heal wounds.

One day, Eliaz proposed a trip to France, to Grasse, to visit her gallery of which she had spoken to him extensively.

In other circumstances, she would have jumped on the opportunity, she would have fomented a strategy signed "Elvira" to draw some advantages from the situation: for example to sign a juicy contract with him, to put him back to work to realize new paintings for the exclusive benefit of her gallery, and thus to relaunch her business by making this Austrian painter of international fame, the very new darling of the jet-set.

In a fraction of a second, here she is in the skin of a moth flying (at the risk of its life), around the warm flame of a lit candle.

This invitation torments her. She thinks about it unceasingly. She imagines her triumphant return to Grasse. She imagines her return to business. She imagines her return to grace after this period of disgrace of which she still keeps a bitter aftertaste.

And then one day, she gave him her agreement in principle.

Yes, you heard right. She agreed to return to France.

Now she had to organize every detail of this escapade in Grasse.

From a financial point of view, Eliaz will take care of everything.

They will go by train. It's a good thing, Eliaz

is afraid of flying.

She has to find a place to stay.

In a hotel? No way. They will have to declare their identity. Too risky.

At her home in the villa? Yes, but the mess left by the workmen does not incite her to propose this solution to her illustrious guest. But after all (she thought), why not?

Her friend the cab driver could summarily put the villa in order before their arrival, but he doesn't have the keys.

Then, without wasting time, she contacted her friend Lucas. The only one she could trust completely.

The next day she took the train from San Remo to Ventimiglia.

At the station of Vintimiglia, she found Lucas who took her to lunch.

She explained to him her project of express renovation of the villa. She gave him the keys plus a well-stocked envelope. There is enough to do with and the remainder will be to thank him for his devotion. They will be able to meet again later in tête à tête if he wishes it.

Elvira perfectly knows how to practice the politics of the give-and-take.

Interesting prospects.

Lucas did not have any difficulty to accept the service that his friend Elvira asks him to return to her, in a perfect discretion obviously.

He accompanies her to the train station, helps her to settle down and kisses her before going down on the platform. Elvira gives him a complicit smile.

The Ventimiglia - San Remo train starts, moves away and disappears from his field of vision.

He joins his cab and returns to Grasse.

54

The day after his return to Grasse, Lucas abandons his cab driver's hat for a while and improvises himself as a site manager.

He goes to the villa and makes an inventory of fixtures.

He has one week to do the job. His conclusions are optimistic. It is feasible, he says. There is not as much damage compared to the fears of his friend. He leaves the villa confident, with the assurance of a substantial profit at the end of the work. At worst he will participate in the restoration work. No question of disdaining the economy of a workman if, he can make himself useful and thus save labour.

He goes to the nearest temporary employment agency and recruits two young construction workers.

The bulk of the work is completed after three days. He releases one of the workers. With the last worker, he fine-tunes the cleaning that was necessary after the work.

This worker seems friendly. He is very young, hard-working. He inspires confidence in him. They discuss a lot.

Lucas ignores that this worker had already worked in this villa, a few weeks ago.

Was it chance or persistent bad luck?

The worker knows a little more about the future occupants of the villa and their arrival date.

At the end of the work, Lucas offers him a bonus.

Everyone is happy. He registers his coordinates for a next mission if the opportunity arises.

At the boarding house, Elvira continues to maintain good relations with Eliaz. They do not leave each other any more.

This meeting seems to have metamorphosed Elvira who (seen from outside) has considerably lowered her guard. She is unrecognizable.

"Hunt the natural, it comes back at a gallop."

The prospect of making a lot of money with this painter she thinks she holds in her hands (by dangling a multitude of benefits if he agrees to partner with her), has rendered her oblivious to the danger posed by her presumed fugitive status, a status incompatible with her intention to return to Grasse.

The mad dance of the butterfly around the warm flame of the burning candle continues. Nothing and no one can stop it.

"Fate blows without a forge bellows," they say.

55

It is a Thursday.

Elvira and her guest, the painter Eliaz, are leaving San Remo for Ventimiglia.

On their arrival, they are expected by Lucas at the exit of the train station. He picks them up and drives them to the villa in Grasse.

Elvira finds her villa with a certain apprehension. She inspects it from top to bottom before inviting her new friend to enter.

She is satisfied with the work done.

The painter (who had been visiting the garden since his arrival) enters in his turn inside the villa.

He is subjugated. He is delighted to be welcomed in this exceptional place, but his wonderment lasts only a moment.

Indeed, he begins to wonder about the real reasons of the exile of his friend and future partner Elvira in San Remo, whereas she possesses this magnificent residence in which, the life seems pleasant. According to him, it is necessary a serious and imperious reason to leave such a house and to go to take refuge in a boarding house in San Remo.

He is not reassured.

His sixth sense tells him to leave this villa as soon as possible and to go to a hotel, but the mysterious charm of his hostess prevents him from leaving.

Elvira offers him to move into one of the rooms upstairs and allows him to have access to all the amenities of the villa.

Of course, open bar 24/24.

357   Elvira PLYNN Greatness & Decadence

What more could he ask for?

The next day, Friday, Lucas is again on a mission. He is in charge of driving them throughout the day after the visit to the painting gallery.

Eliaz is in a complete wonderment. Normal: Elvira anticipates and satisfies all the desires of her guest.

Lunch outside in a gourmet restaurant and dinner at home where her talent as an "unparalleled" cook, finished erasing the last fears of Eliaz.

To complete the picture, he had the right to see the little house dress (revealing fluorescent pearls tied around the waist), her barefoot and the swaying gait between the living room and the kitchen.

Paris: Friday at the very beginning of afternoon.

Robert PLYNN receives a mysterious message.

"*Grasse: case in progress, come quickly!* "

The police station of the 8th district is immediately informed of the arrival of this message.

A quick investigation with colleagues in Grasse confirmed that the villa was once again inhabited.

Saturday morning, 6 am.

On the intercom of the villa, the bell rings repeatedly.

Elvira, who (after a torrid night with the painter upstairs, had just returned to her room to finish her night and take a few hours of rest), had just gone to bed, was startled to hear these repetitive ringtones.

She finally got up. On tiptoe, she approaches the front door.

She activates the surveillance screen.

"*Oh shit!*" she exclaimed.

On the screen, she saw the image of three uniformed police officers standing outside her gate.

The "friendly" young worker knew Andrei personally.

Some would say:

"*It's all down to bad luck.*"

What about you?

END

Elvira PLYNN Greatness & Decadence

Elvira PLYNN Greatness & Decadence